R.K. FULTZ

BAR
girl

ISBN (e) 978-1-7341607-1-0

(p) 978-1-7341607-0-3

Editor—Chell Morrow & Audrey Hughey

Cover Design—T.E. Black Designs; www.teblackdesigns.com

Cover Photographer—CJC Photography; www.cjc-photography.com

Cover Models—BT Urruela, Rachael Baltes

Interior Formatting—T.E. Black Designs; www.teblackdesigns.com

This book is for my Mom, who was an avid reader of romance. I would sneak her novels when I was a young teenager. The day she caught me reading her treasured books, was the day our bond started. Over the years we would trade novels and talk endlessly about characters and story lines. I cherish this connection with her. She passed away due to Dementia. The disease took her memory and the love of reading. We stopped having our book chats and exchanges. One of the last conversations was about me telling her I wanted to write a romance book and she said "you will be great at it because of all the books you have read over the years". She gave me support without question.

Mom you will forever be in the pages of my books.

CHAPTER
one

LIZA

I AM SWEATING LIKE A whore in church. I remember hearing the phrase thrown around to explain how it feels to be in uncomfortable situations.

Lord, I don't know your feelings on me being in this church, but my gut is screaming for me to leave. I keep the thought to myself as I ease my way into the last pew. I want to be closer to the door, but only a few empty seats are available. The funeral service is full, and everyone is sitting elbow to elbow.

Do they feel the same as I do, like a bright light is no longer shining? I don't want to draw any attention to myself since I'm a stranger around this town. I observe folks trying to figure out who everyone is and how they know the girl lying at the front of the church. They may think I look familiar, but I am nobody in this town.

I am Liza Hendrix, a bartender from Berkeley Springs, West Virginia. It's a two-hour drive from York, Pennsylvania, where the funeral is taking place. I've come to say goodbye to Julia Costello, a woman gone way too soon, and the reason I and so many others gather here today. I look around like everyone else, but my attention is not on peoples' faces as much as the flowers sitting in every corner. The overwhelming scent of roses and carnations is teetering on the edge of sickening.

The arrangements vary in size and color, and the local florists outdid themselves, but they make me feel a bit claustrophobic. I'm sure everyone in this town sent their condolences if the multitudes of bouquets on display are any sign. My heart feels the blossoms represent sadness, with nauseating scents. Julia is inside the coffin, and I needed to be here to respect our new friendship.

It didn't take too long to drive here from my hotel. I caught the sights along the way and thought about Julia growing up in this town. Did she leave good childhood memories? Did she have a big family? Did she leave unfulfilled dreams behind? I sit here among total strangers and mourn for someone I spent four hours with two weeks ago. I know all these people in their black clothing and tear-stained faces would not understand why, but Julia would. Her beautiful soul is gone, leaving only her body inside the closed casket up front.

I try to control my breathing as silent tears roll down my cheeks, and grab tissues from my purse. I do my best to control the tears so I don't break down into a blubbering mess. I am dabbing away at my eyes and cheeks as they fall despite my efforts. Julia and I had become fast friends. I divulged to her about my mom leaving me when I was eight years old. She listened when I talked about how my dad never got over her. He became sick pretty soon after she left us, and the doctor diagnosed him with a heart problem. I felt the diagnosis was ironic since he sure did have a broken heart.

I started working at a local bar in Berkeley Springs, Dixon's Last Stand, seven years ago, to earn extra money after Dad went on disability. I recently left there, never imagining I would have stayed so long tending bar. When Dad went on disability because of his heart issues, I knew it was up to me to support our family.

Julia and I had hit it off during her first visit to the bar. The feeling of loss now is overwhelming and makes me want to drop to the floor in front of these strangers, curl up, and cry until I have no tears left. I am broken and miss the friendship we started. Julia had an energy people gravitated toward, and I am one of those people. I miss my friend, the one I was meant to have.

There is movement at the front of the church. I watch a door open and overhear the ladies in front of me whisper, "The family is coming out." I continue to dab the tears from my eyes. My legs are shaking as I watch a couple come first. My whispering friends afford me the luxury of a play-by-play. They say these first two are her parents.

The gentleman is holding the woman close. He is tall and robust with dark brown hair. He appears to be holding up his wife, and she leans toward him for support as they make their way to the front-row seats. The single white daisy the woman is holding in her right hand draws my eye as they turn and take their seats. She gently rests her head on the man's shoulder. The poor woman looks exhausted. I can see her spectacular salt and pepper hair and stylish haircut even from my back-row seat. They are both attractive, despite the pale look of their complexions.

Next, a silver-haired woman using a cane comes through the door and walks to her seat. My not-so-quiet informants identify her as Julia's grandmother. She is using a cane but otherwise looks to be healthy. She is beautiful, and not just for her age, but for any age. Her skin is smooth and shimmers like porcelain, and I can tell she has some makeup on. Her natural glow doesn't hint at her true age, and I wish for that same complexion when I grow older.

Several other people make their way out, including the pastor. I hear the ladies in front of me indicate the final person stepping through the doorway is Julia's older brother. My breath catches in my chest, and I feel an intense vibration coming from him. His dark brown hair matches his father's and sister's, but his short-cropped hair stands out. Julia said her brother served in the military, and his hair is still short, but not to the military standard by any means.

His dark force makes me sweat. I'm nervous—if he learns details from the night at the bar, he would be furious with my atten-dance. A drop of sweat trickles down my spine as he looks into the crowd. I briefly wonder if he is looking at me. He finally sits down as the pastor starts the service.

He and others fill the whole service with detailed stories of how Julia touched many lives. I get the urge to stand up and fill them in on our story. Instead, I remain seated and listen to the incredible music and heartbreaking testimonies. My ears zero in on the last song, which the pastor declares was Julia's favorite. I guess over the past several years I hadn't played a lot of music around the house. This song isn't one I have heard before, so I listen intently as the lyrics explain what it means to let your soul shine. Julia had no trouble letting her soul shine.

This service and her favorite song make me hunger for new music. It is past time for me to expand my world with new things. I make a note on my phone to download this song. At the end of the service, they dismiss the family and others attending from the front first. I sit and watch people go up to place sentimental things on top of her cherry-stained casket, the last goodbye to the one they all love. Her mother leans over and hugs the top of the casket. I feel like I am trespassing on a private moment, and my chest tightens as a panic attack threatens to overtake me.

I stand up and whisper to the folks in my pew that I need to exit. They are gracious enough to give me room quickly, which somehow makes it worse and sparks a new flood of tears.

Just a few more seconds till you get outside, I tell myself, trying to hold it together as I step toward the exit leading to my freedom.

"Dear, are you okay?" a soft female voice asks as I reach the main doors.

I turn around and find the silver-haired lady with the cane, Julia's grandmother. She is sitting in a fancy high-back chair by the double doors leading to the freedom I crave. I have my hand on the door and am one step away from this heartbreak and back on the road. How did she get back here before everyone else?

"Honey, you sure you're alright?" She seems concerned. Here she is trying to mourn for her granddaughter, and yet she is worried about some strange girl. I look at her and pay close attention to two things: her caring eyes and brightly painted, pink-lipstick smile.

"I can't breathe." My hand slides from the door handle as I turn and step toward her.

"I completely understand," she replies. I have a knot in my gut, a fear she knows my secret. It's not rational since I've never met her. Something makes me gravitate to this silver fox. "We are planning to have everyone come to the farm afterward. I can breathe there." She sighs. "You're welcome to stop by if you have time."

I have no idea how to answer her. "Thank you, but I shouldn't intrude." I make my way toward the door again, but she is relentless in a too-tight, warm-hug kind of way.

"It doesn't matter if you knew Julia for ten minutes or ten years; all are welcome. Please, anybody's life she touched, we want them there."

I drop my head and shed a few more tears as I ask her for the address. She introduces herself as Grandma Frankie and gives me directions. I shake her hand before walking to the safety of my car.

Once I am in the driver's seat, I grab the steering wheel and rest my head on it. I came to show my respect for Julia. I wish she could have known the impact she had on me, the lonely girl working nights in a bar, listening to other people's stories of hardship and happiness. The job was a means to pay for my dad's medical bills, and the schedule helped me stay home during the day and offset hours with his personal care assistant. I went through the motions, taking orders and serving nameless faces, trying to keep a smile on my face while working through my struggles at home.

Julia walked into the bar, and she was a whirlwind. I had never met anyone like her before. She caught me off guard with her sense of humor and excitement for life. We were raised in two different worlds but connected by listening to one another. Julia encouraged my dreams, and they had been far off wishes before meeting her. I had never actually shared them with anyone.

I need to learn more about her, and I hate like hell it will be after she died. My mind keeps bringing me back to how I made a huge mistake, and I can't forgive myself for it. Fate had a hand in our paths crossing, but I plan on keeping her memory alive.

CHAPTER

two

THE PARKING LOT IS JAM-PACKED with cars. I'm happy to see it and to hear the music blasting from the employee entrance as I approach. Tonight can't go fast enough for me. I say several prayers to keep the dark thoughts out of my head, wishing not to keep replaying Dad's funeral. I've handled tons of details since he passed away, paying off bill collectors with the remaining money in his accounts. I am fortunate he had enough life insurance to cover his funeral and still leave me a little money for a fresh start. The thoughts are weighing on my mind. I have one more obstacle to tackle: my childhood home.

His accounts and life insurance finished paying the remaining balance on the mortgage. I genuinely don't have the heart to stay in our home. It has never been a happy place, and now that Dad's gone, it's just an empty box of memories. The broken promises echo loudly in every room. The walls of the house are bare, showing his lack of participation in my life. I make my way to the bar and clock-in on the main staff computer, and a loud female voice requests some service.

"How does a girl get attention in here tonight?"

I turn my head toward the sound, not sure who is asking. I find a dark-haired girl sitting at the bar, smiling at me with a wild-eyed look.

"Do I have to flash my boobs at you?" she asks before throwing her head back and laughing like a crazy woman.

Who is this girl? I seriously can't help but laugh along with her. She doesn't seem to have a care in the world, and I realize I would love to feel that weightlessness and carefree spirit. She is still staring at me.

"I am joking with you. No boob-flashing from me tonight."

"I've never seen you in Dixon's before. Is this your first time here?" I drop a napkin on the bar in front of her.

She looks at me and nods. "You are correct, my friend, and it appears I've picked a popular night to meet a blind date."

Damn. She has guts. I couldn't imagine having the nerve to go on a blind date, let alone coming into a madhouse like this to do it.

"What will you be having tonight?" I lean on the edge of the bar and wait.

She shouts her order to me and half the bar. "Let's kick things off with a Long Island Iced Tea." I nod and make my way to mix up her order. "I am Julia, by the way. This seems like a pretty cool bar to work at," she says as she pulls her phone from her purse and starts looking at it.

"Dixon's is the hot spot to hang. It can be crazy some nights, but the owner is great. My name is Liza. What do you do for a living?" I ask as I make her drink.

"Oh, I am a wild-ass farm girl who occasionally parties too much but has dinner with her family on Sunday." She smiles and then spins around and looks at the crowd. Julia is bouncing in her chair. My hope is her blind date shows up soon because this girl is beyond excited. She seems like the type of girl who will talk you into trouble but stay by your side during the whole mess and then help you clean it up. I have the feeling that Julia and I could be friends.

LIZA

I DOUBLE-CHECK THE ADDRESS Grandma Frankie gave me. Although she mentioned a farm back at the church when she invited me, I never imagined the views I would see at the end of the long, tree-lined driveway. A large wooden sign at the entrance indicates it is Costello Farms, and on the sign, there is a gigantic "C" burnt into the wood. I assume it is a brand. The driveway brings me right up to their house, and I notice a huge red barn to the right. I'm amazed because it appears their land goes on forever. I couldn't imagine living in a place with this much freedom.

I park near a bunch of other cars, and it seems everyone from the church is here. You could almost see the makings of a casual barn dance or lawn party instead of a memorial. People are wandering around everywhere. I wait for a few moments in my car and take in the farm. I know you shouldn't judge a book by its cover, but this place looks homey and straight from a holiday movie. It's inviting, and a place where I could get lost taking pictures. The tiny two-bedroom house I lived in with my Dad never held much warmth, and I always dreamed of sitting on a front porch like the Costello's.

Julia's porch wraps around the entire front of the structure. How many nights did she sit here looking at the stars? My dad tried to provide for me, but he failed to deliver the happiness most child-hoods should have.

I am lost in my thoughts when a loud knock on my driver's side window makes me jump. I turn toward the sound and see nothing but a midsection in my face. I take several deep breaths to slow my panic, then pull the door handle and open my driver's side door.

I ease out and put my feet on solid ground before closing the door. When I look up, I am staring directly into Julia's brother's eyes. She never told me his name. My body falls back against the door for support, but I keep my eyes locked on him the whole time.

"Do I know you?" he asks. The ability to speak has left my body.

I stumble around my words but finally reply.

"Frankie invited people to stop by the house." I lock in on his brown eyes, maybe because I couldn't tell how dark they were from the distance between us in the church. His irises are dark and deep, solid black. Does this occur often or only because he appears irritated?

"How did you know my sister?" He didn't budge, waiting for me to speak. I am terrified to tell him the truth and provide the real answer. Our time together is already complicated, and then to add explaining all of it to Julia's brother is way too much for me to handle right now. Besides, he seems annoyed that I am here.

"We recently met and hadn't known each other for very long." I turn and walk away from my car. "It's time I get inside to pay my respects and speak to your grandmother."

I walk away, not giving him a chance to ask me any further questions. God, he makes me feel like I am walking through a freaking inferno. I need to pay my respects and leave. I know I should not have stopped by because my gut is telling me I am an intruder on this family's painful day. I don't want to add to their misery. Their daughter and sister touched my life, and I want to have the courage to share that with her family. The problem is they might ask me a bunch of questions, and then it may lead to how we met. Then the events from the night she died might be revealed and would lead to them knowing it's my fault.

I make my way inside and walk toward the kitchen where it seems most people have gathered. I spot Frankie sitting in a chair at the end of a long, craft-style farm table. It sure looks like it could handle an army of people. We never ate at the dining room table in our home. Dad didn't care for family meals or conversation.

"Hello! Glad you could stop by." Frankie greets me with a smile. My imposter syndrome is raging big time as I smile back at this lovely woman.

I make my way and sit at the end of the table near her. "I want to pay my respects to you and Julia's parents before I get back on the road." I put my bag in front of me on the table. There isn't much in the bag but my pawnshop digital camera and drugstore lip-gloss. I don't have much to show for my life, but this isn't the time to feel sorry for myself. I am alive and simply need to figure out how to begin to live my life.

"Oh, sweetie, did you bring your camera?" She reaches and places her hand on my bag.

"Yes, ma'am." I open my bag and show her my digital camera. It is my single purchase with the money left since Dad passed. I couldn't bring myself to get a brand new one. I guess old habits don't disappear when you get a little money. "It's an old Canon I picked up recently." I smile at her, feeling a bit embarrassed by my older model camera. I think about the new sleek ones, but I love this one. It fits perfectly in my hands, and my heart fluttered the moment I stumbled upon it in the pawnshop. The camera filled me with a warm feeling deep down. Maybe it was my soul trying to shine.

"Have you been taking pictures long?" She looks at me with sincere interest. She has the same dark brown eyes as the guy who knocked on my window, but unlike him, her eyes are twinkling where his burned right through me.

"I guess you could say I have been passionate about photography all my life. I plan to take some courses online and then get as much real-world experience as I can."

She smiles at me and places her hands on mine. "Oh my, you should walk around on our farm with your camera. My grandson would be happy to show you around. There are great places on the farm and one special spot in particular you could capture." She breaks my heart into a million pieces with the idea.

"Who are you visiting with, Gram?" We both look up, and it's the older dark-haired man from the church, Julia's father. I stand up and reach my hand toward him. He places his hand in mine and introduces himself as Anthony Costello. He turns toward the woman he was with at the church, waving her away from a nearby group. She walks toward us and introduces herself as Maxine.

They seem like such big-hearted people, to open their home to basically the whole town. I can tell they are worn down and barely holding themselves together. I know it is time for me to leave and let them all grieve without outsiders bothering them. As I begin to tell them how much their daughter meant to me, the man from outside walks in the room and toward where we are standing. He has changed from his church clothes and is wearing dark jeans and a black shirt with buttons, its long sleeves rolled up. I study the tattoos down his left arm. They have incredible detail in the symbols, and I know there is a story to tell, which explains some of the darkness I sense from him. I have a strong feeling that he is not the sharing kind. His black cowboy boots are beat to hell, yet he makes them look like he could model for a clothing ad.

"This is my son, Jackson."

I reach out and put my hand in his while I take a few seconds to look at his tattoos. They are vibrant black and red. I now see his left forearm is an actual sleeve of tattoos I could stare at for hours. I've always loved tattoos with intricate details, and his sleeve is mesmerizing. I finally introduce myself and stop admiring his body parts.

"Hello, Jackson, nice to meet you. I'm Liza." He didn't waste time with my hand in his. He quickly drops it and then slides his hands in his front jeans pockets. His message is loud and clear.

"Mr. Costello, I'm sorry for your loss. I understand you only met me a few minutes ago, but I would like to offer my help while I'm here. I plan to leave my number with Frankie." Jackson looks uncomfortable hearing this. He shuffles back and forth.

"That's kind of you, Liza. We appreciate you being here for Julia." Mr. and Mrs. Costello both hug me. I know it isn't much, but it seems like the right thing to do. I sense someone staring and see Jackson abruptly turn without saying a word and walk toward another group of people.

I had made no plans to stay, but my conscience has been screaming at me since arriving in town. I give my number to Frankie and say goodbye while looking in Jackson's direction, knowing I will not speak with him again. I yearn for more time with Julia. I need longer than the four hours we spent that tragic night.

CHAPTER

three

JACKSON

THE QUIET IS WONDERFUL NOW, after the whole town stopped by to pay their respects. As the last of them departed, I found my way to the front porch and sit, looking out at the stars. I'm desperate for a few minutes to myself, so I can stop just being polite and avoid the constant formalities with everyone. There are plenty of fake smiles and formal replies of "Thank You," no less than one thousand times. Why would you thank people after someone dies? It doesn't seem right, not to me. Who the hell makes up these rules?

It's hard to know Julia won't walk up the stairs and through the front door. It hasn't really hit me that she's gone. I want to know about her thoughts that night. Why did she get on a motorcycle in the middle of the night? Damn. Julia had made decent choices in her short time, and I never could imagine she would choose to go for a ride that late.

Who was this guy she met up with, and why was she at a bar in West Virginia? I know I need to get answers. My soul won't rest until I learn the full story. Julia was my blood, and I wasn't there to protect her. I went off to war and spent years defending hundreds of other people and allowing them to return to their families, but I couldn't save my sister here at home. The unanswered question is why she ended up on a stranger's bike all the way in West Virginia.

Julia usually spent the night with friends if she planned to party and hang at a bar. The soldier in me needs to get the answers my family deserves. I have supported my parents since Julia died. I haven't left their side yet, but I need to go to West Virginia and get those answers.

Thoughts of Liza keep creeping into my mind while trying to figure out the details of Julia's death. I met most of Julia's friends, but this girl I don't recognize. She appears to be in her late twenties, which would put her around Julia's age. Liza is intriguing, with dark brown hair hanging down past her shoulders. I have several crazy thoughts about gently tugging it.

I envision myself and Liza outside the barn. I sneak up on her taking pictures, walk over and kiss the back of her neck after running my hands through her luscious hair. She would wear a tank top showing skin and baring her gorgeous neck. I daydream about kissing a bare shoulder and moving up her neck.

My body wants her body to ease back against mine. I didn't miss the warm amber color of her eyes when she shook my hand. Is amber a real eye color? She's shorter than my 6 feet and 2 inches. I don't know how short, but I don't feel there will be any issues with our bodies fitting together.

Shit! I don't have time for a relationship or a hook-up with someone passing through town. My heart has been ripped out, and yet my dick doesn't care, because it's screaming for attention. I glance at the barn.

"Julia, you had plans to get this place noticed and help the farm thrive. You had a plan, little sister, and you failed to share it with me before you left."

Mom and Dad had asked us to come up with a new marketing strategy. They wanted to increase sales without spending all their time working on our dairy farm. They had given me the green light to promote my equine therapy program. I am on board with the idea of a new website and marketing plan, but I need Julia. She went to college for marketing and had connections around town. She called and left a message the night she died, saying that she found a photographer to help.

I am not sure how to move forward, but this farm needs growth and exposure, or we are at risk of shutting down. We've been showing a steady decline because several new farms in the area have a better social presence. Costello Farms might be the largest in southern Pennsylvania for Equine Therapy, but we need to advertise.

I'll talk to everyone tomorrow to see if they have any ideas. I know Grandma Frankie always has an idea. She is a force of nature. I wish to be half as invigorated as she is at her age. I also need to inquire more about Liza and see if she can give me details on her background. She is a stranger around here, and yet I feel she did know Julia. My instincts are kicking in and telling me that she is hiding something, and I need to protect my family. I couldn't protect Julia the night she died but now is my chance to make things right. I owe it to them.

CHAPTER four

"HEY, THIS PICTURE IS BREATHTAKING. I don't understand why you are serving drinks."

I turn around fast and spill a little of the beer I was about to serve.

"What the hell?" I yell at Julia as she holds my cell phone in her hand. I checked my phone earlier from habit and then chastised myself for doing it. I guess you don't change habits just because someone dies. This has been routine for me every night I work, to check on Dad and the nurse who stays to see if they need anything.

I had laid my phone down to help someone at the other end of the bar, and Julia must have picked it up before the screen locked. She has some nerve.

"The pictures on my phone are private, and you can go right ahead and set the phone back down." I'm pissed. We just met, and she has the nerve to look through my phone.

I clean up the splashes of beer I spilled and try to stop freaking out over the fact she looked through my private photos. It probably reflects my lack of confidence in my pictures, and I am embarrassed right now. I'm nervous someone might say my photos are worthless. The emptiness has been there so long, and I keep myself emotionally shut off since dad got sick.

"I am not playing with you. These pictures are remarkable. I feel like I could stand right there with you. Liza, I am not a professional, but this picture captures a sensational moment." She lays my phone down.

I walk over and stare at the photo. "Do you honestly believe it's any good?" I ask Julia. She looks me right in the eye and grins big, then nods her head without hesitation.

"I know you met me like five minutes ago, but cross my heart, I am telling you the truth." She crosses her heart with one hand. "Liza, you need to be doing this for a living." Julia puts her hand on mine and taps the photo. I look at her and raise my eyebrows, my mind flipping. "I know some people who could use your help. I have connections."

She winks at me and takes another sip of her drink then looks down at her phone. "Well, my blind date will be here in ten minutes. We have a few more minutes for girl talk."

I roll my eyes. I guess she feels I am there to provide her company. I honestly didn't mind, but I still have a job to do. I try to listen to her while working at the bar. She tells me she lives a couple of hours away in York, Pennsylvania.

I want to ask more about these connections she mentioned, but I worried I might sound needy. It's exciting to get a chance to take pictures, and I am okay if it's a one-time thing. I'm working my nerve up to ask her if she is legit, but then Julia shares the news that her date is here. She checks her hair and makeup in a little mirror she pulled from her purse.

"Here goes nothing, Liza. This could be my future coming through the door or my next big mistake!" She laughs and asks me for another drink. I shake my head at Julia but laugh along. I think about how fun she is as I fix her next round.

Liza

THERE IS SO MUCH INFORMATION swirling around in my head after meeting Julia's family. My overwhelming guilt and wanting to tell her family how I know their daughter weighs on me. Julia's family is grieving badly, and I want to help them, but I am walking a fine line. Would they forgive me if they learned the truth about me being Julia's bartender that night?

Julia was my opposite in every way, and it made our new friendship extraordinarily unique. We shared stories and hit it off like sisters. She gave me her phone number, and we planned to talk a few days afterward about her business proposal. I didn't have any other prospects and wanted to do something different from working nights at Dixon's. My passion is photography and has been since I was a little girl. I kept it hidden for the most part from my dad. It seems like a cruel twist of fate has brought me here to continue this journey and finish what Julia wanted me to do.

The sun is coming in through my hotel window. The room is outdated with dark-stained wood furniture and plaid curtains, but the queen-size bed didn't sleep badly. I packed my car with a few belongings when I left Berkeley Springs. I brought my comforter to help me sleep in a strange place. I was exhausted last night and not sure it would have mattered. When my eyes finally adjust, I grab for my phone and notice the time is 9:02 a.m. My stomach rumbles loudly.

There are a few cafe-style places I remember passing yesterday, and my stomach is signaling the first thing on the agenda is breakfast. My taste buds are craving a plate of French toast with a side of bacon. Yesterday was hard enough, but losing my appetite didn't help because I am feeling the after-effects this morning. My head is aching, and I am starving. It is time to take a shower and grab some food. I spoke up yesterday and told Julia's family I plan on staying around for a while. The town is a great place to get pictures, which will help with downtime until I can get with Frankie.

My phone vibrates as I begin to rise out of bed and put my feet on the floor to stand up. I look down at the screen and see that it is a Pennsylvania number. I push the button to answer.

"Hello, this is Liza."

"Liza, this is Frankie. Did I wake you up, dear?" A familiar warmth comes over me. Frankie has some sort of magic power.

"Hello, Frankie. How are you this morning?" I stand and walk toward the window as I wait for her reply.

"I am good, thanks for asking. I want to see if you might have some time to come by the farm this morning. I have a small project I would like to discuss with you." I pace the floor. This sounds like the conversation I had with Julia at the bar.

"What type of project?" I ask, my curiosity overwhelming me.

"Well, to be honest, I would like to talk with you in person if it's okay." My heartbeat speeds up. I am nervous about going back to the farm, but I couldn't refuse Julia's grandmother.

"It's fine. I do have to shower and grab some breakfast. I can be there at eleven. Does that work?"

"That's perfect," Frankie replies. "I appreciate your coming to meet me." We both say goodbye and hang up.

It's starting to get crazy. Julia is pushing me to help her family. I know I offered and want to honor my offer, but what happens when one of them asks me how I met her?

Jackson still worries me. I feel like he can see right through me. It sure seemed like it yesterday at the farm. There are many pieces to this puzzle, and I need to put them in the right places to see the whole story. I worry I won't have enough time to figure everything before the truth comes out and my part in her death is revealed. I hate to admit this, but I want to know a bit more about Jackson. His intensity draws me in. I want to know about his life before Julia died. I felt sparks the moment we touched hands yesterday. Did he feel anything?

There are dark storm clouds in those eyes, and I understand that empty feeling since my dad passed. I had a fleeting moment of wanting to ask him if I could help, but I knew it would be a waste of time. I still want to take my chances and do it, but I am way too scared.

I bypass all the little cafes and choose the full-on diner experience this morning. I find a place called Ruby D's, and it turns out to have the best French toast I have ever eaten. After breakfast, I pay more attention to my surroundings during the drive to the farm. This town is stunning. I saw quite a few farms similar to the Costello's. It would be quite therapeutic to get lost on the back roads taking in all the farms and countryside. I bet there are a bunch of old houses and barns I can capture with my camera at daybreak or sundown.

It's part of my dream to be a photographer. I would love to go on day trips around my town roads in Berkeley Springs and find old abandoned houses. The screensaver on my phone captures the scene right as a storm rolls in. The clouds are full and dark, threatening to burst above a rundown and dilapidated general store I found. It is a crumbling shack now, ruined by unforeseen circumstances. It hit me that we share the same state: broken.

CHAPTER *five*

"FRANKIE, I THINK YOU HAVE the wrong girl," I explain to Julia's grandmother as she sits across from me on the front porch. I look around, trying to gather my thoughts and feel the air's humidity as the temperature climbs on this sunny day. The Costello's have an assortment of outdoor furniture set up throughout the wrap-around porch. Frankie and I sit on the west side in a shabby but sturdy set of black wicker chairs. I think these chairs suit Frankie's style. As she pours us both a glass of tea, it all seems to be part of a plan meant to charm me. I am confident she gets what she wants. I don't mean this in a bad way, but she's damned determined.

"I'm certain you are the right woman for the job." She smiles as she eases back in her chair and sips her tea from a small, delicate cup painted with pink roses. I sit silently, my nerves on edge. "Liza, we need your help to save this farm. I talked to my son and daughter-in-law, and they explained that we are long overdue for an overhaul to our farm social media accounts. We need more of a presence, and that includes getting updated pictures of the farm and adding them to our accounts for people to see." She sets down the teacup and hands me a pamphlet describing the farm.

I read it. The pamphlet markets Costello Farms, but it is definitely outdated and not anything you would see today.

"Jackson handles running the farm with his father. Julia had fresh ideas and recently convinced her parents and Jackson to make some much-needed changes." I hand her back the pamphlet.

"Do you know what changes Julia had in mind for your farm?" I want to know if the changes Frankie mentions could be connected to what Julia briefly shared with me. What are the odds both Costello ladies are asking me to help with the same project? I sip my tea with the weight of this on my mind. Drinking also gives me more time to collect my thoughts.

I came to learn more about Julia and help her family. I'm not sure if I can perform the duties for this kind of project, but my soul screams at me to try. I am intimidated as hell, and it's a big deal. I'm worried about the secret of how I know Julia, praying like hell it won't come crashing down on me.

"Liza, did you bring your camera with you?" Frankie asks me.

"Yes, ma'am. My bag is in the car." I look at my car and back at her.

"Why don't you grab your camera and then head around the farm and take pictures. Get a feel for the place and come back and share some of your pictures with me. We can talk about the next steps after. Does that work for you?" She sips tea as she waits for my answer.

I stand and move to the railing so I can look at their land. It makes me feel at ease. I wanted to walk around and see the places Julia loved and feel her spirit while I am out there. I also couldn't ask for a better day to take pictures. There isn't a single cloud in the sky, and I would be a fool to argue.

"Frankie, you win."

"I'm not trying to win." She smiles. "I have a feeling you're the right person for this job, and I can't wait to see your pictures. Please, go explore, take your time. You have my number if you need anything. I am here all day." I walk with her into the house, carrying our tray with glasses and a tea pitcher.

She gives me suggestions on where to take pictures around the farm. The main barn is where I want to go first, and I love the fact that it's painted red with white trim. I run and get my camera from my car and walk toward the barn. I am enjoying a sense of happiness I haven't felt in a long time. I dressed comfortably for this visit, with jean shorts, black low-top converse tennis shoes, and my favorite light-blue v-neck tee shirt. I am ready to explore.

CHAPTER
six

JACKSON

I'M WORN OUT AND MY day isn't even half done. I am working alongside a few farm hands today and have been since 5:00 a.m. Costello Farms is trying to run a normal schedule since Julia died, but the last few days were filled with planning her funeral, and it has put a strain on everyone. The farm is a self-sufficient dairy farm providing products locally and has been in my dad's family for three generations, but I recently asked my parents to add equine therapy.

We have more than enough space with a few extra barns, plus a large corral for training. I've been working with animals all my life and trained working dogs in the Marine Corps. During my first enlistment, they selected me to attend military police training after I completed combat training. During those years, I became a military working dog handler, and it was during that time that I endured the loss of many men. My unit would search in buildings and vehicles for explosives.

My canine partner, Maverick, had my back and I had his. We spent four years together and were called upon for way too many search and recovery missions. I applied to bring him home with me upon my departure from the military. It didn't happen. The Marines always perform an exit physical on all animals before leaving with their handlers, and they found out he had cancer. Maverick's loss still weighs heavily on me because he relied on me for everything.

I switched from my initial plan of canine therapy to equine therapy. My heart hurt too much and couldn't imagine working with another dog. I spent a year down in Charlotte, North Carolina at an equine therapy school. It was amazing to see the kids connect with the horses and do things they may not get a chance to otherwise. The kids may not handle everyday tasks like us, but therapy makes them whole for a few hours. Sharing time with them is special, and it may have been the only thing that kept me on this earth during those dark times.

I utilized the training I learned with Maverick and started helping a local group of kids a few months ago. Costello Farms offers kids a chance to experience therapy riding. I want to provide vets with a chance to participate in the program too. I know it saved me from tumbling down a dark tunnel. Julia was a big part of helping me build the program. I'm constantly searching for her and wishing she would walk around the corner of the barn at any moment.

As I'm thinking about Julia, I see a female walking towards me, and for a split second, I think it's her. Then I look away and toss a bale of hay onto a pile I've stacked. My heart knows it isn't her.

"Damn, this morning keeps getting better." My words are filled with sarcasm and mixed with lust. Liza is walking my way wearing a killer pair of shorts. Why is she here, and why do her legs have to look freaking fantastic? Luckily, I don't say the last part out loud as I grab my shirt off of the edge of my truck. It's hot as hell, but she doesn't look like she's sweating. Her blue shirt fits her body perfectly. Lord, I'm being tested today. I want so badly to keep staring as she walks toward me like a dream, but my lower half will give me away if I do. I don't believe Liza would appreciate me glaring at her breasts or legs.

"Jackson, good morning," Liza says, standing directly in front of me while nervously tucking a strand of dark hair behind her left ear. I stand there, silent. "Frankie asked me to visit today and work on a project with her." Liza stares and waits for my response. I could tell she is nervous; she should be. I don't have time to play games with her or my grandmother.

My grandmother doesn't know her but invites her to work on a project.

"No," I bark, then say nothing further. I watch her step back. I know I scare people; I was trained by the best.

I turn and walk to my truck and climb inside. I look at her as I start my truck up and drive toward the main house. Looking back in the rearview mirror, I see Liza standing there with her eyes on me. I figured I would see tears or hear yelling, but there was only sadness.

We lost Julia, but she looks like somebody as broken as we are. What the hell is her story? I head to the main house and pull into the driveway. Frankie is sitting in her chair on the front porch, waiting for me. She knows I'm not a fan of her projects.

"Sure took you long enough, Jackson." She chuckles as she sips her tea from her favorite rose cup. Frankie loves her tea. There's no doubt she's the definition of a southern belle. She married my grandfather and moved to Pennsylvania, but Frankie's originally from Georgia. You can take the girl out of the south, but you can't take the south out of the girl. I love her.

"Please tell me about this scheme you are cooking up with Liza," I ask as I sit down on the porch's top step.

"Liza was a friend of Julia's. I want to help her. She seems lost." Frankie slowly sips on her tea. She keeps tipping her head and looking off in the distance toward the fields. I hate when she gets the yearning for missions because half the time, she pulls me into them and she's hell-bent on seeing them through.

"Do you know how Julia met Liza?" I look up from where my hands have been rubbing the top of my jeans. I miss Julia, and it still feels wrong to talk like she is in the past.

"I don't know where they met or how, but the first time I spoke with Liza at the church, she was heartbroken. That's enough for me."

I grab a small twig from the step and twist it. This is precisely how I feel inside about this whole situation.

"She's an aspiring photographer. I asked her to take some pictures around the farm today. If she's any good, she can help you with the website." I feel my throat getting dry. I hate to admit it, but I could use some help. The issue is my help was supposed to be Julia, not Liza. I don't have time to figure out what happened to Julia and work with this woman.

I know I've lost this battle today, and Frankie's determined to help this stranger. I'm getting tossed into the middle of it, whether I like it or not. I stand up and walk to my southern belle, bend toward her and plant a kiss on her cheek.

"I'll follow along for now, but I'm going to watch her. If I don't like how she handles herself or if she puts our farm in jeopardy, I'll gladly escort her off the property myself." Frankie agrees.

CHAPTER *seven*

JULIA AND LIZA
DIXON'S LAST STAND...9:45 P.M.

JULIA'S DATE COMES THROUGH THE door, and he's tall with blond, short-cropped hair. His face lights up as he makes his way from the front door toward her spot at the bar. I'm several feet away from where Julia is sitting, but I can still see the sparks flying between these two.

He bends down and hugs her, and I see her whisper something in his ear. Their backstory is none of my business, but I feel there's more to this "blind date" than Julia is telling. My views on love are jaded after several years of working here at Dixon's. It is hard to find a deep and emotional attraction to someone who makes you lose all sense of time and gives you full-body shivers just by being close. But I might be a witness to something like that now.

Dixon doesn't pay me to people-watch, so I get back to serving drinks. I try hard to keep my mind from drifting, but it goes to the past feelings of being trapped for years and a desire for a new beginning. I've sent a few emails to local realty companies to find a buyer for my family home. I'm unsure about our house's worth but hopeful it is enough to provide a little cushion so I can leave town.

"Hey, bar girl. You planning to help us?" I turn toward Julia and wipe my hands on the bar towel, clearing the cobwebs from my mind.

"I know what Julia is drinking, but what about you?"

"Well, Liza, my incredibly handsome date here is Paul, and he wants a soda." Paul reaches to shake my hand and then pulls a barstool up beside Liza.

"Nice to meet you, Paul. Just a soda tonight?" I ask as I fix their drinks and glimpse them interlocking their fingers together. They leave their hands on the top of the bar briefly intertwined, long enough for me to see.

"Yes, ma'am. I'm driving my motorcycle tonight. I always keep sober on nights I'm driving my baby."

Julia rolls her eyes and laughs as she bumps her shoulder against Paul's. "Do I get to see or perhaps take a ride on this infamous baby?" I put their drinks down on the bar in front of the lovebirds.

"What kind of bike do you have?" I ask as I wipe the bar. Julia stares at him with adoration as he explains.

"I'm a motorcycle mechanic here in town, and the shop also does restorations. Mine is a 1991 Fatboy Custom Harley Davidson, and I just got her back on the road," he replies with a huge look of satisfaction.

"I would love to see your baby during my break," I say.

He agrees. It has always impressed me when guys can fix things and use their hands. I think it's hot. Julia seems to feel the same way because she hasn't taken her eyes off Paul since he started telling me about his bike. Julia is holding his hand tight with a dreamy, far-off look in her eyes. Have I ever had a far-off dreamy look in my eyes? When my camera is in my hands, that is probably the only time I have the same dreamy look. My camera provides my only daydreaming opportunities in life.

LIZA

JACKSON DOESN'T KNOW ME, so why does he think he can tell me to stop? I'm furious at this moment and want to punch something. Too bad Jackson isn't here right now. I've decided to get rid of my anger on several haystacks sitting in the barn's corner. I actually land a few good punches and a dropkick or two. My anger management session lasts around fifteen minutes.

I try to shake everything off and head to get some pictures around the farm today. The barn isn't the place for me, in case Jackson comes back to yell and make me feel like a child again.

Well, you threw a tantrum and kicked the hay bales, ass, I tell myself as I make my way outside the barn and head toward a corral. Costello Farms is breathtaking, and there's so much activity happening. I want to capture all of it. Julia's parents must have been an essential support system in her life, along with Frankie.

I decide the jury's out on Jackson.

I quickly notice someone working with a horse in the corral as I approach. I stay back a step, making sure they don't see me. This provides me a chance to capture some candid pictures while they work. The horse is magnificent as he gallops around. I haven't been around many horses, but he is large and has a shiny brown coat and blond mane. The person in the corral suddenly leaps on the horse's back, and I don't see a saddle. He rides the massive animal, and it doesn't look like it's his first time.

They ride around, and I continue taking pictures. I use my zoom lens to get great images of the rider and horse. I'm in shock when I see Jackson in my viewfinder. His face takes me by surprise, sitting high on this glorious animal. I didn't know he could ride with such power, and it appears he's training the horse. I need to ask Frankie about the horses.

The young-looking horse tries to buck him off, and I can relate to the feeling, especially having dealt with Jackson. I roll my eyes, but I don't want to miss any shots. I love the way they seem to fight with each other but give respect. My shutter hasn't had a break since I made my way to this spot.

My camera moves around the arena. Other horses are walking about, and they are just as powerful as the horse Jackson is on. I lose track of him. When I take pictures, I focus intensely on my subject and don't pay attention to my surroundings. I suddenly feel someone standing behind me. I don't need to turn around to know it's Jackson.

"Did you enjoy the show?" he asks, breathing heavily. I turn to look at the man I saw up on that beautiful horse. He's mesmerizing.

"Please, don't pick a fight with me right now," I reply. He walks up beside me and touches my arm to stop me from walking away.

"I talked with Frankie. She clued me in on the project. I'm not totally on board, but I'm willing to try this wild goose chase until it proves to be a big waste of time."

I clutch my camera tight, knowing it holds pictures close to my heart, and they are not a waste of time. I hate feeling like I don't measure up. It brings me back to my childhood. My mom left me when I was eight years old, and at times I feel like the same little abandoned girl. I won't allow him to make me feel like a waste of time.

"Who gave you the authority to tell anyone they are a waste of time? Your grandmother asked me to help, and in my book, that gives me more than enough credit." I respond and wait for the fireworks. He puts on his baseball hat, and I see he has on a different shirt from earlier. It sure looks good with his hat, jeans, and boots. Damn, this man can wear a pair of jeans. His legs look solid and long, and it's all I can do not to jump into his smart-ass arms right now. I imagine it would feel amazing to wrap my legs around his waist. His hotness is such a distraction, especially after watching him up on top of the horse just minutes ago.

Now, I can't get the images out of my brain. I've seen the strength in his legs when he was training the horse and working it around the corral. I want my body to be held up against a wall as I keep my legs around his waist, those sturdy legs supporting me. I can imagine the temptation of his mouth, and I want to let it possess mine. I try to shake the dirty thoughts from my head. Why am I imagining him like this? He can't stand me.

He crosses his arms. The shirt sleeves are short, showing off his tattoos. I love the dark tribal designs coming from under his shirt sleeve, then spiraling into several detailed pictures around his lower forearm. The tattoos add to my attraction to him. He's an egotistical ass, but a hot one.

"Jackson, I don't owe you a thing. I'm here to help your grandmother and honor Julia in the process. Please back off!" I try shoving him as I pass by, to show him I'm not intimidated, but this man is a mountain. He doesn't budge, and I lose my footing in the process. He grabs me to keep me from falling. As we make contact, there's an electric current flowing through my body. I actually shiver.

I've had a nervous habit of chewing on my bottom lip if I get anxious during an uncomfortable situation, and I didn't realize I was doing it until Jackson says so.

"You can tug on your luscious lip all you want, but I'll figure out what the hell you're doing here. You and that lip have been warned. I'm not backing off," he growls but doesn't let go.

I look at him as he gives a wicked grin before throwing his arms off of me. I turn to grab my camera bag and leave, reacting with intense anger and leaving him a lovely parting gesture, a one-finger salute. The effect I am going for doesn't work. I hear a deep sexy laugh as I walk away. Why does his laugh have to sound sexy?

CHAPTER

eight

Liza

I DIDN'T STICK AROUND YESTERDAY after my encounter with Jackson. He got to me. The man puts me on edge, and it's causing me significant issues, like my-panties-possibly-disappearing issues. Jackson has killer forearms, and after I watched him work with the horse yesterday, the images kept swirling in my brain. Dangerous images.

A vivid dream from last night involved Jackson picking me up and tossing me in the bed of his truck. We are lying on top of some hay, which gives us plenty of cushion for the pending activity. I guess I know why the hay played a part in my dream. I remember the popular song playing on the radio in his truck telling a story about a heartbroken guy who runs into his high school love and dreams about a future with her. I've always liked the song, so catchy, desperate, and dream-filled. The windows are down in the truck, and the song is carried through the night air as we lay in each other's arms. It would be hot and damn satisfying. The lust-filled night would satisfy me, but not with Jackson. This man is suspicious of me, and here I'm picturing us banging in the back of his truck.

He is trouble. Julia offered me a sign to move forward, and I don't need to mess it up with dirty thoughts of her brother. After I met Julia and we discussed working with each other, I hoped that she would give me the chance to live out my far-off dream. Once I learned of her death, it crushed me. We connected and started a fast friendship. I know if Julia were here right now, she would laugh at my craziness.

I never envisioned her guiding me after her death. *Julia, I could use some insight into your brother. Do you know how much of a stubborn ass he is?*

My camera bag and laptop are all loaded into my car. I'm off to Costello Farms to show Frankie my pictures from yesterday. I spent last night narrowing the selections and editing the best ones. Costello Farm is vast, and the magnitude of its operation is incredible. I could use a few days to get more pictures and do the whole farm justice. Frankie mentioned we would discuss her project after she views my photographs. I have my fingers crossed because my brain has formulated ideas on how I can help.

After pulling in and grabbing my laptop and camera bag, I make my way toward the main house. I make it to the top of the stairs, and right as I raise my hand to knock on the screen door, I hear several voices in a heated conversation. The voices are coming from inside the house and they have me frozen in place. I can't move. I shouldn't be listening, but I can't help myself. Mr. and Mrs. Costello are talking with Jackson, but it is his voice I hear the loudest in the conversation.

"Dad, I know it's painful, but we need to know why Julia was in Berkeley Springs. We need to get more information on the bar and her date," Jackson stated.

"I agree. The whole thing doesn't make sense. I'm concerned she might've been hiding something," Mr. Costello said. "But I don't want to dig up her dirty laundry and tarnish her memory." There was sorrow in his voice.

I'm glued to my spot, listening for more.

"What do you think happened? Do you think there is more we don't know or something the police haven't shared with us?" Mrs. Costello asks.

"Mom, I'm honestly not sure, but my gut is saying yeah, there's more to it. I feel strong enough to head to Berkeley Springs and that bar for answers," he replies, his voice full of anger.

My chest hurts, and I'm not sure if it's a panic attack or because I've been holding my breath. I could hear every word of their conversation. My time with the Costello's is ending. I need to speak to Frankie and explain my friendship with Julia before Jackson finds out the truth. I'm deep in my thoughts, and I miss hearing the end of their conversation.

The next thing I know, the screen door opens and a hard body crashes through it. Jackson slams right into me with his whole body, knocking me to the porch. My laptop and bag go flying, and I try reaching for anything to stop the motion, while he tries to grab me. My back hits the floor, and his body lands on mine, forcing the air from my lungs as I land.

I feel his full weight on top of me and try to push him off. He is looking down at me and staring right at my face. His expression might be mad, but his eyes show something else entirely. Temptation.

"Liza? Are you okay?" he asks me but doesn't move.

"I am fine. You knocked the wind out of me when you knocked me down. You can get off of me now," I respond, still trying to push him away. He suddenly dips his head, and I feel his breath against my neck. He is lingering there, and it feels terrific. His dark hair is right by my face, and I stare at his soft waves. I can feel his morning stubble as his breath hits my neck, and I desperately want to raise my cheek and rub it against his stubble.

"Why were you blocking the doorway?" he asks, and my desire is quickly doused. I snap from my lust-filled trance.

Jackson stands up. I'm left in my position on the floor.

"I stopped by to talk with Frankie, but you burst from inside like the whole place is on fire." I reach my hand toward him for a little help up and he takes it. I stand up, and he pulls me closer, right up against his body. "Oh," I say as we touch. I'm completely caught off guard as our bodies fit up against each other.

"Liza, why are you still hanging around my family's farm?" he whispers right into my ear. The feel of his body doesn't dull the pain of his question. I want to answer him and tell him the truth, but I can't risk his rejection.

"Liza, I didn't know you were here." I pull away from Jackson as I hear his mother's voice. Mrs. Costello opens the door and comes to my rescue. I grab my bags off the floor.

"I hope it's okay. I'm here to see Frankie." I make my way inside before Mrs. Costello responds. I need to get far away from Jackson right now.

"She's in the kitchen. Please come in."

I walk farther inside and don't look back. I'm on the verge of telling Jackson why I am in York, and at Costello Farms.

CHAPTER

nine

JACKSON

THE DRIVE TOWARD BERKELEY SPRINGS does nothing to cool my temper or the fire burning inside. Liza is a mystery for sure, but her body is something I know how to solve. She isn't what I need right now, but she is what I crave. My body can still feel hers lying beneath me. I can still smell her scent. Liza's presence lingered on the porch long after she went inside. Every moment I spent out there was filled with the sweet hint of vanilla, and it will bring me back to that moment.

I wanted to lick her neck and sample that sweet smell and so much more. The vision of me undressing her right there on my parents' porch and sinking deep into her was overwhelming. I didn't care that my family was inside. It took my mom showing up in the doorway to bring me to my senses. Why does this woman stir me up so?

I don't know a damn thing about her, except she's a knockout. Her eyes hold a deeper story. They are tortured and scarred. That's something I can relate to. There's one thing for sure, I'm not good at dating, and definitely not right now.

My focus is on learning how and why Julia died. I miss her more than words can convey. Julia would punch me on the shoulder and tell me to get my head out of everything and go with my gut. She ran with life, and I'm afraid that's the reason she died.

I can't move on without knowing how she spent her last few hours on this earth. My soul is shattered because I couldn't protect Julia. I've got to know if my sister was living her final moments the way she wanted.

Julia spent her last hours at Dixon's Last Stand. She was there with a guy named Paul Simmons. After several hours, they left on his motorcycle. I checked around since her death, and they didn't go to college together. I've never heard of the guy. I assume she met him at the bar that night, but that's out of the normal for her. Julia wasn't the type of girl to run off with a stranger, especially not after drinking. Julia had a wild streak, but she was never reckless.

I figure the best place to start is Dixon's to see if anybody remembers any details. They might have security camera footage they can share to help me understand how Julia met Paul.

It takes two hours to drive from York to Berkeley Springs. My encounter with Liza left me on edge. It also doesn't help that I plan to talk to the owner at Dixon's Last Stand. I select some tunes for the road and roll my truck windows down as today's memories start to fade while the scenery blows by.

It is not long before I'm pulling into the town of Berkeley Springs. Mom and Dad would bring us to Berkeley Springs State Park and let us play in the famous mineral water as kids. Julia and I loved to play in the water because it was warm, but Mom loved it for the benefits to her skin.

Now, as I think about it, she looks fantastic for her age. I guess the trips worked after all. I was in town one other time a few years back for a guy weekend. A former Marine buddy rented a cabin at Cacapon Resort State Park for a few of us veterans. We spent a weekend there and fished, hiked, and played golf. It was a great weekend, and I don't recall taking a weekend off since. We only went into town one time during the whole weekend because the lodge at Cacapon had such great food. When we ventured into town, I remember there being multiple local restaurants and tons of trendy looking shops all along Washington Street.

Dixon's Last Stand is at the end of Washington Street. When I pull into the parking lot, my heart is pumping faster than usual because I know I'm going to walk through the door and ask for details on Julia's last moments. My throat is dry. If I don't go in there, my parents would be okay with letting things go. We could move on.

The reality is my heart hurts too much to let it go. I walk toward the front entrance in no real hurry. The dread weighs heavily on me. I hesitate a second before pulling the handle on the door and heading inside.

Dixon's bar appears clean and is styled in wood planking from the floors to the ceilings. The planking is rustic-looking cedar and has a distressed feel. I look at the dance floor, which also has the same style but with a few more boot scuffs. I walk to the wrap-around bar and look up. A hanging sign indicates Dixon's serves lunch and dinner, which is perfect because I am starving. It's not crowded, but I guess it is early for the usual bar crowd.

There's a tall guy with salt and pepper hair that doesn't look old enough to have it happening yet. He has a few days of beard growth, also sprinkled with gray. He is working on the other side of the bar but notices me as I sit. He grabs some silverware and makes his way back.

"Welcome, man. I'm Dixon. Can I grab you a beer?"

That is music to my ears. "Yes, please. I'll have a local beer on tap."

He smiles and steps over to pour my beer.

"You passing through or staying here in Berkeley Springs?" he asks.

"I drove down from York, Pennsylvania for the day. Doing some business in town," I respond. He sets my beer in front of me. I take a sip and it tastes like heaven.

"You might stay here a little longer if the storms hit us. Keep an eye on your weather app before you head home. I'll be right back to take your food order," he says before he walks away.

I grab my phone and check the weather to see there is a significant storm heading this way. My trip started with no actual plan so I could sleep in my truck tonight if need be. It wouldn't be the first time. I turn to look out the bar's windows and notice the storm brewing outside. Maybe I can make it back before it gets cranked up. I didn't pack a bag or anything because I had full intentions of returning home after my visit. My nose picks up a mouth-watering aroma making its way from the kitchen, and it gives me another reason to stick around: a delicious meal.

Dixon walks out from the kitchen to my spot at the bar. "Do you know what you would like to eat?" He has his order pad ready.

"Can I get a cheeseburger with the works?" I ask as my stomach rumbles loudly.

He nods. "Comes with fries. You good with that for a side?"

"Hell, yes. I'm starving." I grin as he writes my order, then clips it to the kitchen window's circular order wheel and spins it for the cooks. I keep working on my beer and look around. There appears to be one waitress working the floor along with Dixon at the bar. I guess at this time of day they don't need a full staff.

Dixon has a stage in the back for bands and several small tables scattered around the dance floor, and pool tables in the far-right corner. There is a bunch of motorcycle memorabilia on the walls, and it's not surprising with his appearance. I'd guess a lot of his patrons are bikers. It sure makes me miss my old bike.

I haven't been on it since being discharged from the Marines. The joy was gone since leaving. After losing many friends and my service dog, I had no interest in riding. Now, I miss the feel of the bike and freedom.

Julia always asked me to take her for a ride. First, she was too young. Then, when I got back, I didn't have the heart to ride anymore. She asked me one time since being back on the farm, but I told her my bike was in storage and needed a tune-up. I never took it in for a tune-up and got her on the bike. Could I be the reason she climbed on the back of this guy's bike?

"How was everything?" Dixon asks, breaking me out of my thoughts.

"It was excellent." I wipe my mouth and place my napkin on my plate.

"Would you like another beer?" he asks as he picks up my plate.

"Yes, sir."

He nods as he carries my plate away and walks to pour me another. I decide it is finally time to ask questions.

"Dixon, you have a minute to talk? I have a question."

He sets my beer down. "Sure. Ask away." He leans against the bar and waits for me to continue.

"Well, a couple of weeks ago there was a young woman in here that left with a guy on his motorcycle, and they were in an accident. I want to see if you remember her from that night." I start nervously.

He stood up and ran his hand through his hair. He suddenly appears older than my first impression of him.

"Man, it was a horrible night and one I'll never forget. We take pride in helping our patrons get home safely. I've got a program with discounts, and I work with a ride finder app to help people find safe ways home. The bar provides space for the patron's vehicles to park until they can safely pick them up." I could tell he takes drinking and driving seriously. "The police gave me a final report and confirmed she left with her date on his motorcycle, but he hadn't had a drop of alcohol. I talked with my bartender, who served them both." He was shaken, and it is terrible to see him like that, but this was crucial to helping me find answers. He quickly turns the questions on me. "Why do you ask?"

It took a moment to keep my feelings in check before answering. "The woman on the back of the bike was my sister, Julia Costello." The color drains from Dixon's face and he drops his head. He appears to be collecting himself, but then he steps toward me and extends his hand. "I'm extremely sorry for your loss," he says with deep sorrow in his eyes.

Dixon appears to be a respectable business owner and from all the news clippings posted on his walls, a well-liked local biker. I will not leave him hanging. I place my hand in his and shake.

"Jackson Costello, and thanks for your sincerity."

I feel a slight tremble in his hand. I am sure the conversation is not easy for him either. This biker might have a gruff exterior, but inside he appears to have a big heart.

"I know my words mean little to you, but if there's anything I can do for you or your family, let me know," Dixon offers. I proceed carefully with what I want to know next.

"I'm trying to learn about her last hours and why she came here that night. I know you said she left with a date, but we didn't know him. Do you know if he was from the area?" I took another sip of my beer, hoping Dixon knows more about this Paul guy.

"I had seen him in here a couple of times but didn't know him. He worked as a mechanic here in town at the bike shop." I paid close attention to this new information. Did Julia find him attractive because of his link to motorcycles? I guess my next stop is the bike shop.

"Dixon, you mentioned the police talked with the bartender who served them. Does he or she work tonight? I would like to talk to them if possible."

He shook his head. "I'm sorry, but she no longer works here."

Damn, just my luck.

"Okay. Could I leave my number to pass along when you talk with her again? I want to ask her a few questions." I added my cell to the back of my business card from the farm and handed it to him.

He holds my card and reads it. "I can pass it along, but I'm not sure if I will see her again. She left town after the accident. Your sister's death messed her up."

"I understand. Would it be possible to get her name? I know I'm walking a fine line with privacy issues, but I have to try."

"I can't give out personal information, but I do promise to pass along your business card whenever I see or hear from her again." He extends his hand one more time.

I don't hesitate to accept it. I figure my last question might earn me a fast exit. "Is there any way I can watch your security footage from that night?" I hold my breath for his response.

He ran his hand across the top of his head again. "I would show you, but my business has been slow for the last few months, and I had to cut some costs. I still have my cameras, but they are set up to record for twenty-four hours, and then, unfortunately, the footage gets recorded over the next day. I'm sorry, Jackson," he answers, but it looks like it's the last thing he wants to say.

I am defeated as I pay my bill, and figure I can at least make my way to the bike shop. I want to try to learn more about Paul. I check the weather app on my phone to see how much time I have before the storm starts. The app still shows I have time to head down the street and visit the bike shop.

It takes about five minutes to drive over, and right after I get out of my truck, I notice a sign in the window indicating they are closed for vacation. It appears they won't open up again until next week. I take a few minutes and peek inside the windows. The first thing I see is the office area. It has a waiting room with chairs and a customer service counter. The area looks professional and orga- nized. There are decorations on the wall and plants in the corners. I walk to the bay doors and look through the windows and see several motorcycles sitting in various states of repair. The business looks clean and state-of-the-art.

I open my phone and search the web for the bike shop's name and discover that two ex-military guys own it. The shop has been open for six months and has excellent reviews. They specialize in repairs and restorations. I am curious if Paul was an owner. I grab another card from my wallet and add my cell and a note on the back as I did at Dixon's. Maybe between the card I gave to Dixon and this one, I will get a call and get more answers about the night Julia died.

I recheck my weather app and figure it's best to head home before the bulk of the storm hits on my drive. Will Liza still be at the farm working with Frankie? Maybe I should hang back at Dixon's and find a one-night hook-up to get her out of my mind. I consider it for roughly one minute, but my thoughts go back to her body underneath mine on the porch. I climb into my truck and start my two-hour trip back to the farm. I'm a lost cause in more ways than one.

CHAPTER *ten*

JULIA AND LIZA
DIXON'S LAST STAND... 10:30 P.M.

D IXON'S IS PACKED, BUT IT didn't stop Julia and Paul from dancing. I'm busy working but catch a glimpse from time to time. Julia gives the appearance that she can take care of herself, but I still keep watch when I can spare a second or two. My instincts tell me she's hiding some details here and there. I like her date so far. My first impression is he's a genuinely nice guy.

I understand about family secrets, and I didn't tell Dixon anything about my dad's health issues once I was employed here. He offered the daily lunch shift to me several times, but I always turned it down and told him I liked nights best. Dad's health declined the day Mom left us. She met someone else, and we didn't fit into her lifestyle any longer. I ran over my childhood in my mind and the day she left us. My childhood stopped when Mom walked out of the front door. Although the weight of a sick parent is off my shoulders, the sadness from both of them hangs on tight.

After a ten-minute break, I head to the bar and steal a glance at

Julia and Paul. They're on the dance floor wrapped in each other's arms. It's obvious to anyone watching them that they have feelings for each other. I believe they fit together well. He's listening to her every word and holding her close while dancing. Paul's hand is draped along her lower back while his other hand is entwined with hers, pressed close to his heart. The scene is exceptionally intimate for a first date, let alone a blind one.

Julia hasn't permitted me and she might get mad, but I want to capture this moment. I take my phone from my back pocket and make sure they're in focus. He's holding her like he doesn't want the night to end. This picture could be a memory they'll cherish. I double-check the shot. It's gorgeous, and I note Julia looking up into Paul's eyes. I quickly snap the picture and capture them falling in love.

Liza

"These photos are stunning. I am blown away you were able to take these pictures in just a few hours on our farm," Frankie exclaims. She is excited as she clicks through them on my laptop. My nerves have finally settled down after my front porch interlude with Jackson. Sitting here with Frankie is enjoyable, and I'm shocked she loves my pictures. We're sitting at the dining room table I love as she goes through all my pictures. Frankie's opinion matters to me, and the fact she seems excited makes my heart soar.

This is the first time I've ever been asked to take any photographs specifically for someone, and for a special purpose. I tried to capture the genuine feeling of this farm while I wandered around the property, getting a true sense of the family.

I learned the farm has been in the Costello family for three generations. Anthony Costello makes the third son running the farm, and from all the stories the staff shared, they're happy

working here. I turn to Frankie and raise the biggest concern everyone, including myself, seems to have.

"I have learned quite a lot from being on the farm already, but
many people who work here are nervous about Jackson's plans to
take it over from his father."

Frankie pauses at the laptop and rotates in my direction.

"Liza, I honestly don't know. My son has brought the idea up to
Jackson several times since he came home. He tells his father he isn't
sure. He isn't ready to commit to anything in his life." Frankie
shrugs and gives me a half-hearted smile as she turns back to the
screen.

She suddenly gasps as she stops on a picture I took of Julia's
special place. Frankie shared the details of the location; Julia would
often head to this special spot for peace. When I was there to take
pictures, I loved Julia's choice of location. It was off the main path
from the rest of Costello Farms, near the back of the property by
the lake. There are lots of trees and bushes surrounding the area,
and it has a small overlook to the east of the lake. The overlook
divides the land between the Costello's and the neighbors'
properties.

Frankie shared that Julia went to the overlook and sat for hours
to look at the lake and the rolling farmland. I admit to connecting to
the overlook. It was a quiet place to talk to Julia. I could almost hear
her laughter.

"I believe you and Julia shared a special friendship. Am I wrong?
It may have been new, but it was still special," Frankie says as she
puts her hand on top of mine. She smiles, and I feel like I can trust
her. She stops looking at the laptop and focuses on me.

"Yes, ma'am. We met recently and connected right away." I held
my tears back and kept a smile on my face. I tried to recall those
first few minutes when we met. Frankie chuckled a bit and leaned
back in her chair. "She was wild and I am the complete opposite,
but we hit it off. She helped me figure out I have more to offer than
just working at the bar." My instinct is to spill everything I know
from that night, but my nerves keep me from saying anything more.

"Julia was always headstrong, right from the beginning. Since the moment Anthony told me they were expecting a little girl, she has been a handful." It doesn't surprise me. I enjoy hearing about Julia's childhood. "She was a free spirit and had many hysterical nights related to curfew and boys. Julia loved to ride horses, and she wanted to travel. The two biggest things you should know are: she didn't know a stranger, and she loved this farm." Frankie is proud and heartbroken at the same time. Her granddaughter meant the world to her.

"I have a job offer for you if you're interested," Frankie says as Maxine walks into the room.

"Frankie, are you starting without me?" Maxine grabs a chair and sits down beside Frankie to look at my laptop screen.

"Max, you'll understand why I'm going to offer Liza a job here on the farm. Look at these pictures from yesterday."

I don't say anything, but I'm anxious about this offer she has now mentioned twice.

Frankie turns toward me again and shares information on the anticipated growth of the farm. "Anthony and Maxine have done a marvelous job with the dairy side of the farm, and it still survives after all these years. The problem is a few other dairy farms have sprung up in the last few years, and they have a more prominent social media presence. I am not about to explain it all to you, but the bottom line is we need your help in creating new marketing material and updating our website. Julia was in charge of marketing and hiring a photographer."

I sit in shock because I'm the photographer. Julia was telling me about a special project, and my gut is saying this was it. My anxiety is building because they want me for the same project as Julia. I'm feeling overwhelming guilt, and I need to step outside before I have a panic attack. I would hate for Frankie and Maxine to witness my meltdown.

I stand up. "Would you excuse me for a minute? I need to grab something from my car." I didn't give them a chance to respond. I hurry down the hallway toward the door, the hint of fresh air urging me on faster, along with the desire to get in my car and drive away. My vision is blurry with tears, but the door is finally right there. I hear it open and see a blur of color just before I collide with something. I crumble from the force, but at the last minute, two strong arms pick me up. Jackson lifts my body as if I weigh nothing and makes it look effortless for him. I move my hair away from my eyes to look at his face, and he stares back at me with compassion. This is a completely shitty day.

He always seems to catch me at my worst. I can feel his heart beating. Damn, it is going as fast as mine. My mouth is open, but there is no sound, and Jackson senses my anxiousness. He turns from the house and carries me down the steps before heading toward the barn. I look up into the sky as we make our way to the barn, gazing up at the dark clouds and realizing a major storm is brewing. I feel exactly like that right now on the inside and know it will break loose. The tears I worried would fall come as predicted. I want to scream and thrash like the storm is going to do real soon. Does Jackson have to be near me and watch it happen? I need to let my feelings out but hate that he might witness my storm.

CHAPTER
eleven

LIZA

JACKSON STILL HAS ME IN his arms. He carries me to the back of the barn, where we go through an open doorway into an office. He shuts the door with his boot before he takes me to a sofa along the far wall. Jackson keeps me in his arms the whole time as he slowly lowers us down onto the sofa and holds me on his lap. The storm is ramping up outside the barn, and the heat is escalating inside. I hear the thunder vibrate off the walls, and some pictures shake. My nerves are on maximum overload from the storm and being in Jackson's arms. He pulls me towards his chest and lets my head rest on his shoulder. He doesn't say a word, and my tears flow from this gesture.

I'm unsure how long we sat in silence, or how much time passed before my tears stopped, but I do know I enjoyed the scent of leather and wood. His cologne is terrific and fits him perfectly. I close my eyes for a minute and feel Jackson's hands in my hair. His touch is delicate as he works his hands down the length of my hair. I keep my eyes closed because I don't want to break the spell.

I listen to both his breathing and the storm. The sounds are mesmerizing. The wind picks up, and there's a loud crack of thunder. It breaks the spell. I sit up and notice Jackson's left arm lying on the couch, my favorite arm. His left arm has complex life stories, inked down over his veins. The bold black with splashes of woven red draw me in. I wish I knew the tales that inspired all of his tattoos. Why did he mark his skin with these forever stories?

The woman in me has always found full sleeves to be primal and full-on sexy. I imagine Jackson grabbing the side of my hip and making me his next chapter. I look up into his eyes, black as midnight, and his hands slowly untangle from my hair.

"Do you think the storm will last much longer?" I ask.

He doesn't blink and answers me with a question of his own. "Do you mean the storm outside or the one between us?"

I'm caught off guard and unsure how to respond, or if I even have the ability.

I try to reply, but Jackson doesn't give me a chance. His mouth is on mine and it instantly feels like heaven. He slides his tongue inside my mouth slowly and it begins to dance with mine. In my dreams, I imagined how Jackson's mouth might feel when it could consume mine, but my dream didn't include his scent or moans. Jackson could make a fortune selling recordings of his moans because they're deep down in his throat and sexy as sin. I feel them vibrate against me.

I don't want this feeling to end and know I need to stop it. His lips are worth throwing it all away, but I can't do this without him knowing the truth. For Julia and her family, I need to do the right thing, as hard as it is. Lord knows it's hard right now. Jackson's body is made to make a woman scream all night, and I haven't screamed in too long. I pull away from his luscious mouth and ease my way off his lap before standing on my own two feet.

"Liza, what're you doing?" he asks me while adjusting his jeans.

"I need to slow things down, Jackson. The thoughts of Julia, and now with us working closely. It's a bad idea," I explain and straighten my clothes. It gives me a chance to get my lust in check. He stands up and asks.

"What do you mean working closely?" I'm amazed at how fast he fixed his clothes.

"They have asked me to help Costello Farms with website updates, new farm pictures, and to help create new marketing material. Frankie and your mom offered me the job today."

His face is red. "I assumed my grandmother wasn't moving forward with this project, but it appears I'm wrong." He runs his hands through his hair, then looks at me. "I guess we'll see each again." He nods and walks out.

CHAPTER

twelve

Jackson

M Y FAMILY NEEDS TO EXPLAIN the hiring of Liza at the farm. Many scenarios are running through my mind while dressing for breakfast with my parents. Their house is a quick drive down the hill, and I want to catch all of them together to get answers. I also needed to fill them in on my trip to Berkeley Springs yesterday. I tried sleeping after my encounter with Liza, but being with her had been hot as hell, and I hate to admit it, but I didn't want it to end. Liza turns me on, and I can't do anything about it, not long term.

The thought that I might not be able to offer her anything more than a night of meaningless sex doesn't play well for me. Liza is for sure a long-term commitment woman, and I almost had us twisted up in a one-night stand. My focus should be on Julia and getting to the truth of her last hours. My family isn't helping my cause by asking Liza to work on the farm.

I climb into my truck and remember Liza's breakdown yesterday. It brings back my memories of anxiety after leaving the military. It was a large part of why I got involved with equine therapy, which helped me heal and bring purpose to my life. Julia often told me the love of a good woman could add life back into me, but I dismissed her. I would even reply with, "I'm not a one-woman man," but deep down, I know I am.

I pull into my parents' driveway and make my way inside. I catch the scent of bacon the moment I enter the door. I'm starving but also anxious to get this morning started.

"Hey, Son. You sure picked the right time to visit. We're sitting down for breakfast," Dad declares as he pulls his chair up to the table.

Frankie is carrying fresh biscuits, and I can see she's dressed as usual, ready for the day. I don't know how the woman does it, but she looks radiant every day, with today being no exception.

"Jackson, I'm glad you joined us this morning, we've got plenty," Mom says with happiness in her voice.

I need to make my way here for breakfast more often.

"This looks and smells fantastic. Trust me, it won't go to waste," I reply. I sit down at the table and then look over and notice a playful side-eye action between Mom and Frankie. It sure looks suspicious. "Is there something happening with you two this morning?" I ask as I fill my plate with eggs, bacon, and biscuits. My dad looks up from his plate as I ask the question.

"We are curious if you know how Liza is doing this morning." Frankie looks directly at me. Oh Lord, here we go, I figured these two would dig for news.

"I assume she's okay, but I haven't talked with her this morning. Why do you ask?" I respond, throwing it back to them. I take a moment to shovel food into my mouth, and it gives me a good reason not to answer any more questions.

"We saw that you and Liza were spending time in the barn yesterday evening during the storm and wanted to make sure she got home safely," Mom replies.

Well, there it is! Dad is suddenly interested now, and looks between us all, waiting for someone to respond.

"Mom, we were stuck in the barn because of the storm and

hung in there for a while, but finally made a break for it and went home separately." Frankie and Mom appear disappointed. "I stopped by this morning to find out who hired Liza to work here on the farm." I look at Frankie and Mom while taking another bite of my breakfast.

Dad finally joined in the conversation. "Maxine, what've you and my mother been cooking up besides breakfast?" he asks. I suspect he didn't know Liza would be working on the farm.

"Jackson, your grandmother invited Liza to take pictures around the farm, and she's talented. We offered her a job to help build our social media for the farm," she explains to Dad and me.

Frankie stops eating and looks at us both. "She'll provide a fresh perspective and will help you, Jackson, with the marketing for the equine therapy program. Besides, I feel Julia would be happy knowing her friend is helping us." Frankie was good at delivering a punch to the heart.

"I respect both of your feelings, but do you know anything about her background and if she's qualified to help us?" I ask them both. I pick up my plate and walk it to the sink to rinse it.

"Jackson Costello, why are you so distrusting? There's no harm in giving Liza a chance. Son, seriously all you need to do is look at her photos. You'll feel the same way we do. She's one hundred percent qualified." My mom is standing near me, and her hands are on her hips.

I'm in trouble.

When my mother uses my full name while addressing me, along with putting her hands on her hips, it means I have lost the battle.

"Fine, but if she skips town without a word, just remember I didn't agree with hiring her." They all nod in agreement. I figure it is a good time to tell them about my trip yesterday. "I drove to Berkeley Springs yesterday and stopped in at *Dixon's Last Stand*. I met the owner and spoke to him about Julia." I walk back to the table and sit down.

"How was Dixon with all your questions?" Dad asks.

"He was receptive, and you could tell Julia's death impacted him." They look hopeful. "I asked him if I could see his surveillance footage, but unfortunately he didn't still have it. It gets recycled every twenty-four hours." I see their disappointment, but I keep going. "He told me Paul was a bike mechanic at a local shop in town, so I left my card. I'm expecting to speak with them next week," I explain. "Dixon also said he would pass on my card to the bartender if he saw her."

"You think there is any chance Mr. Dixon can get in touch with that bartender again?" Mom asks. "It would be great if you're able to ask her some questions. It still doesn't make sense for Julia to hop on Paul's bike," Mom states.

The problem is the three people we desperately need to ask are gone, Paul, Julia, and the elderly truck driver who pulled out in front of them. The police and paramedics claim that the old man had some medical emergency right before the crash, which is why he pulled in front of Paul. He may have been trying to drive himself to the hospital. He has no immediate family around to ask questions. It leaves too many unresolved issues and questions.

"My investigation has not ended, and I plan on going back to the bike shop next week to ask more questions about Paul. I want to learn more about his background," I share with everyone.

"Thanks for driving all the way there and talking with Mr. Dixon. I know it wasn't easy," Dad chimes in and puts his hand on my shoulder. That's a big gesture for him.

The daily chores call my name, which is good because I don't know how much longer I can keep my emotions in check. I tell everyone goodbye and head straight for some fresh air.

CHAPTER

thirteen

"HOW ARE YOU GUYS DOING?" I ask ascI approach the side of the bar where Julia and Paul found seats, and they both face me.

"I believe you're slacking a little," Julia says, showing a mischievous grin.

"And why do you think I am slacking?" I ask as I hand a customer sitting near her a drink. Paul laughs.

"We both should have our next round here waiting on us since we're your favorite customers! What should I do with this girl?" she jokes.

I shake my head because she is simply over the top, and Paul laughs at us both.

"I'll take another soda, and my girl will have a big glass of water." Paul gives their order before giving Julia a kiss, then steps away from the bar. Julia didn't argue with him ordering her water.

I figure it is my turn to tease her. "It appears my favorite customer has been cut off by her blind date." I laugh while getting their order.

"Make jokes, bar girl, but I want to ride on his bike, and he won't let me if I'm drunk. I hate to admit this, but I do want to ride home with him, but I'm nervous," she explains.

"Have you been on a motorcycle before?" I ask as I set their drinks down.

"No. I used to beg my older brother to take me on his bike, but he never would. I want to go home with Paul, and the idea of being on the back of his bike, that's intoxicating." She rolls her eyes. "I know, lame, but truthfully I had imagined my first ride would be with my big brother, but here I am whining about how a hot guy is offering to take me home on his bike. I should not have any other thoughts but him and the night ahead." She looks sad.

"Julia, I don't know the whole story about your brother and why he never offered to take you, but from my observations, Paul seems like a great guy," I offer. I'm not sure if it helps, but at least her smile is back.

"I've got a break coming. Do you two want to step outside for some air and look at Paul's motorcycle?" I ask.

"Let's go," Julia replies without hesitation. Paul is walking back toward the bar, and Julia fills him in on us going outside. He agrees, and we make our way through the crowd and feel the cool air hit us as we open the door to the parking lot.

Paul leads the way to where his motorcycle is parked on the west side of Dixon's. It's a thing of beauty. I don't know much about motorcycles, but Paul has done an impeccable job of restoring this one.

"Paul, this looks amazing. I am blown away," Julia says.

I whip my head around and take in these two for a second. "I guess this isn't your first date, and for sure not a blind date." I look at them as I mention the information Julia had shared.

Paul smiles at Julia. "I guess we haven't hidden it well. We do sort of know each other." He laughs as she walks to him. "Julia called my bike shop and asked for help restoring her brother's motorcycle."

I am stunned at the revelation.

She wraps her arms around Paul. "My older brother has a motorcycle he hasn't been on for quite some time. I wanted to surprise him and get it running again. The bike meant a lot to him at one time, and my goal is to encourage him to rediscover that lost part of himself. I want to bring back his joy of riding," she finishes before Paul kisses her.

I am touched she would do this for her brother.

"I researched bike shops away from town since I want it to be a surprise," she explains. Paul chuckles, and she continues with the story. "I was lucky enough the day I called that he answered the phone."

"I agreed to handle the job as a side project for her," Paul chimed in. "It would have cost her a lot more if I ran it through the shop. I had a buddy drive and pick it up with his wrecker. Tonight is our first face-to-face meeting."

I'm in awe of these two.

He is blushing as she speaks again. "I'd call to check the status of everything, and he would call me back with questions. Soon our conversations focused less on my brother's bike and more on us," Julia replies, still holding onto Paul.

"Julia, this is such an incredible thing you planned for your brother. Is the bike finished?" I ask.

"Yes. I finished the work, and we planned to bring it to her family's farm this week. We decided to meet tonight and work out the details," he explains, and Julia beams with satisfaction.

Her brother better appreciate all these two have done for him.

LIZA

IT TOOK ME THREE DAYS to get my affairs in order after I agreed to Frankie and Maxine's offer. I went back to the main house after

Jackson abruptly left the barn the other night and dropped off a note in the doorway to tell them I accepted. I also said I would begin as soon as I got settled. My next order of business was to find a small place to rent, hopefully something already furnished where I would be allowed to pay on a month-to-month basis. I only need a place to sleep and cook a meal, not to entertain or stay long.

I paid a visit to Ruby D's for lunch and found her putting up a sign to rent an upstairs apartment above her diner. The apartment is small, and it was her place before she married the local hardware store owner, Earl. They're both widowed and found love again. As luck would have it, the apartment is furnished, and she readily agreed to rent it month-to-month, especially after I offered to help at the diner if she needed any extra hands. When I explained I was working at the Costello Farm, Ruby revealed she is a friend of Frankie's, and I know it helped me. I felt lucky stopping in there for lunch, or maybe it was Julia's handy work.

After I settled in and began my research for my new job, I decided it is time to show my face at Costello Farm. I'm not sure how to dress for this type of work. I want to look presentable but not too formal for being on a farm.

Admit it, a nagging thought whispered. *You also wish Jackson would give you a look or two.* I put on my best-looking dark jeans and a tight-fitting, long-sleeve red top with black faded heart imprints. After pulling on my knee-high black boots, I donned my silver necklace and matching hoop earrings. My hair is hanging loose today, and I spray it to get a beachy wave look.

The drive from my new place to Costello Farms isn't much shorter than from the hotel. I love the scenery and could get used to this every day. After I park my car and walk up the porch, the first person I see is Frankie.

"Good morning, it's good to see you. I'm happy you agreed to do this project." She hugs me, and I have to admit her hug calms my nerves.

Three days had passed since I'd seen Jackson, and I'm not sure how he will behave for my first day working on the farm. My nerves are ramping up with anticipation as I think about it.

"Maxine will be down in a minute and can take you to the barn."

I stiffen with memories of the barn. I sure don't need her to notice.

Frankie grabs my hand and leads me toward the kitchen. "I would walk you there myself, but I've got a friend coming in a few minutes. You know Ruby. We're going shopping and then having lunch."

I guess she has heard about my new place.

"Ruby's wonderful. She is letting me rent her small upstairs apartment, which is perfect for me," I reply as Maxine walks into the kitchen.

"How marvelous, Liza. Glad you found a local place, and you can't beat my best friend." Frankie pats my hand as she walks with me to the doorway. "I'm glad you are sticking around and helping us on the farm." She smiles at me.

Maxine walks toward us. "Let's head to the barn." I nod in agreement, and we all step onto the porch. Ruby's already in the driveway, waiting on Frankie. She waves at us and honks her horn. I wave back. We walk down the stairs and make sure Frankie gets in the car okay.

As Frankie and Ruby leave, Maxine and I walk into the barn and head to the back room. I spot a sofa along the wall. I could feel the heat creep up my neck. "This is our farm office. We fixed it up a few years ago, right after we learned that Jackson was returning." I look around the room at three desks, each set in front of a wall and the sofa pushed into the empty spot along the far wall.

We both stop upon hearing footsteps and turn as Jackson walks into the room. He looks relaxed and has an iPad under one arm. He shouldn't look this good. He wears a pair of worn cowboy boots, light-colored jeans with some holes here and there, and a green work shirt. The work shirt is worn, and I have no doubt this man works hard on the farm. I can imagine my body rubbing up against the worn fabric of his clothes.

Liza, get your mind focused, girl.

He looks up at his mother and me. He frowns and sets his iPad down on the desk.

Would he be okay with me ripping the buttons off the front of that shirt?

"Why are you ladies here this early?" he asks as he crosses his arms.

"Jackson, we discussed this the other day. Liza is here to take new photographs of the farm and your equine program. She has settled in town and is ready to get started. You could catch her up on the marketing plan Julia started." Maxine holds her ground while Jackson inhales and uncrosses his arms. He walks to his mother and hugs her.

"Mom, I'd be happy to show Liza around the farm." He says and then looks at me. "The problem is, I don't anticipate her fancy boots lasting one hour," he jokes, staring at my killer black boots. Now Maxine is looking at my boots.

Oh, no. Maybe these boots weren't a good idea

"Jackson might be right. Please tell me what size you wear?"

"7 and a half," I answer. I didn't bring any other boots, and I would hate to waste time going back to town.

"Jackson, we have extra boots here in the barn, and she is the same size. Can you help her find a pair before you show her around?" Maxine asks. I can see his jaw clench, and I guess they must be an old pair of Julia's boots. This morning is not going well at all. Damn. "I'll catch up with you both later," Maxine says before leaving us alone in the room.

He stares at me. "Didn't make the best choice of farm attire on day one, did you?" he finally asks. I looked down at my outfit and saw nothing wrong with it, except maybe my boots for running around the farm.

"I didn't think through my boot situation," I admit.

"We do have mud and muck around every corner here. I'm not sure where you come from, but I would guess it must be paved with good intentions instead of hard work," he spouts off before walking away.

If it weren't for the fact that I haven't told him any of my past, I would smack him with the truth on how damn wrong he is. *Jerk.*

When he walks back into the room with a pair of boots in hand, I am ready for him.

"I'm glad you have me all figured out, Jackson. Not that you care, but I assumed we would be indoors more today," I replied. He doesn't say another word as he hands me the boots. Julia's work boots.

"When you finish lacing up, meet me outside to begin your tour and tutorial," he orders and walks toward the door. I don't let him get far.

"This isn't an assumption but more an observation. You are not happy I am here, are you?"

He stops mid-stride. "Liza, I don't need the distraction," he blurts, then continues walking outside.

I finish lacing up my new work boots and head outside to meet him. He's waiting in his truck, so I climb in and Jackson begins filling me in on Costello Farms' history. I figure I'll leave his earlier comment alone for now. We drive around the property for hours, and I get to see every inch. I also get to talk with several farm hands during the tour. I am on farm-overload by the end of the tour. His family has built an impressive business.

We head back to the barn office. Inside, I grab my other boots and figure out my lunch plans. Jackson mentioned he needs to get a few papers off his desk.

I'm still lost in my thoughts on his earlier comments about me being a distraction. I've had time to roll it around in my brain, and it has only added fuel to my fire. I assume I'm a distraction in a good way, or maybe a bad way. I might need to run an experiment.

After I grab my things, I walk to where Jackson's desk is on the other wall and invade his personal space.

"Excuse me, but can I borrow a pen and a piece of paper from you?" I lean against his desk, waiting for him to hand it to me. He rolls his eyes but grabs both items and gives them to me. I rub the side of my hip and thigh against his arm as I reach for them. I feel him tense up. Interesting. I must still affect him. Is this good or bad?

I use the paper to fan myself as I stay right there by his desk for a second. He hasn't taken his eyes off me the whole time. He looks uncomfortable, and I'm not sure why, but I like the fact he is. I'm playing with fire, and I know I'll get burned.

"Liza, do you need anything else? He asks with fire in his eyes. He flipped my switch the other night when I was vulnerable, but I honestly can't afford to get involved with Jackson. I give him a wink and turn to leave the office.

Please leave it alone, I tell myself. *We need to work together, and my craziness isn't helping that situation.* I make it to the door when I hear his voice.

"I'm heading to town for some supplies, so you will have time for lunch. Liza, please be warned: The next time you try to play with me here at work, I'll throw your fine ass right up on my desk and have you screaming my name in no time." He winks at me and then leaves before I can utter a word.

CHAPTER

fourteen

JACKSON

LIZA IS OFFICIALLY DRIVING ME crazy. I mean this in a pure "battle of the sexes" way. We have been continuously side-stepping each other for the past two days, around the office, in the barn, and all over the farm. Ever since the other day, when I warned her about teasing me, she turned things up a notch. She has found every excuse to step to my side of the barn. It will be the need to borrow office supplies or discuss farm details, and we've had lots of time walking the property together. Liza always wears jeans that show off her killer curves. I think it is time to take a break before I make good on my threat of laying her across my desk.

Today, I inform her she'll be on her own since I'm heading out of town for business. Liza didn't ask questions, which was good. I wasn't up for sharing the details of my trip. It's hard enough to discuss Julia's death with my family, but even harder with strangers. I received a voicemail yesterday from the owner of the bike shop where Paul Simmons worked. He said they would be open all week and to stop by anytime to talk. I figured it was time to pay them a visit and ask some questions about Paul. I still want to see if they know anything from the night of the accident. I called earlier to make sure the shop owner would be here today.

The other reason for the trip is Liza. The side-stepping around each other is making me insane. We've covered all the basics of farm life. I've got to admit that she has impressed me with her attention to detail, studious questions, and endless curiosity. I gave Liza a task to give a presentation on the information she has researched on how we can get the Costello Farm brand rolled out. I figure the best way to learn is a trial by fire, and it will show her sincere interest in helping this farm. She appears enthusiastic, but tomorrow will confirm her enthusiasm.

I pull into the parking lot at the bike shop. The sign in front reads "Berkeley Bike and Restoration." I make my way through the main doors and a guy standing at the counter looks up.

"Hello," he says. "How can I help you?"

"Yes, can I speak to the owner? I left my card last week."

He nods. "Sure, he's in the back." He gestures for me to have a seat in the small waiting area to the left. I sit down and wait as he disappears into the shop.

They have a small waiting area, but a big coffee service with lots of supplies. I guess the customers love their coffee. I'm not a big coffee drinker, but maybe a cup here or there if long nights at the farm demand it. The wait gives me a chance to check my phone for messages since I left Liza working on the presentation. She may have a question and couldn't contact me.

Well, no messages or missed calls. I guess she can handle things. I'm not sure if that makes me happy or not.

"You asked to speak to the owner? Is there something wrong?" I hear a deep, booming voice and look up to see a guy standing near me with a uniform shirt on. He's probably 6 feet or taller with jet black hair cut in a military style. He's built, and I assume from hours in the gym and hard work here at the bike shop. I'm not great at guessing age, but I would put him around 35 years old, which would make us the same age.

I stand. "The name is Jackson Costello, and I would like to see if you have a few minutes to talk about Paul Simmons."

He crosses his arms and assumes a defensive stance.

"What's your interest in Paul?" He is intimidating, but I don't scare easily and I wasn't backing down.

"My sister Julia was with him on the night he died. I am trying to learn more about Paul and see if you might know anything more from the night they died," I explain, holding my ground.

He tips his head back for a second and looks up at the ceiling before responding.

"I'm sorry for the loss of your sister. My name is Will Green-field." He extends his hand to me, and I quickly respond with a shake.

"Will, thanks for the kind words. I hate to disrupt your day, but I need more information for my family's sake. It was suggested by the owner of *Dixon's Last Stand.* He said you might be able to help me with some background information on Paul." My anxiety eased a little now.

"Let's head back to my office for more privacy," he suggests. I nod in agreement. Will gives me a quick tour of his shop as we head back, and the place appears to be a top-notch operation. I'm feeling once things settle down, I might bring my motorcycle here. My bike needs a tune-up, and I have this new sense of urgency to get it back on the road.

Will opens the door to his office, and I follow him inside. After he shuts the door, we sit down.

"Julia was on the back of Paul's bike the night they died. My sister had not mentioned Paul before the accident. I want to learn more about him and try to figure out the timeline on how and when she met him." I lean back and cross my legs. My stomach is doing flip-flops.

"Jackson, let me say I am extremely sad to learn what happened with Paul and your sister. Paul was like family to me, and I know in my heart it was an accident. If there were any way he could have avoided the truck, he would have."

My heart stopped beating. This was not what I imagined I was going to hear. I was prepared for things like, "he was a jerk" or "how could he be so reckless?" In some warped way, that would have made the pain more acceptable.

"I know the police said the older man driving the truck pulled in front of them, and that Paul had not been drinking. But why were they out so late?" I ask.

Will shrugs. "Jackson, your guess is as good as mine. Paul was my best friend, and he was my business partner Gideon's younger brother. I've known him damn-near his whole life, and he was a good kid," he replies with misty eyes. Will pulls a handkerchief from his back pocket and wipes his eyes.

"Gideon shared the police report with me. It explained why the old man driving his truck pulled in front of them. The old man had a heart attack and was on his way to the hospital. The police ruled it an accident."

I know there is utter shock on my face, and Will notices.

"When did you find out he had a heart attack?"

"Gideon called me two days ago and gave me an update. You didn't know he had a heart attack?" Will asks.

"We heard the old man had a medical emergency of some sort," I concede. Why did three people have to die senselessly? "Is Gideon around? I would like to ask him a few questions, if possible." I want to meet Paul's brother, and it was worth a shot to ask.

"I wish he were here. I would give anything to have him here, to support him during this difficult time, but he's more of a silent part-ner. Gideon has other things to deal with right now."

Will stands. I get the sense there's more to Gideon's story, but Will is obviously done with further discussion on the topic.

I take his cue and stand, and we both walk out of his office.

"Thanks for your time and for showing me your business. I appreciate everything," I say as I extend my hand in his direction. He accepts my hand and shakes it.

"Jackson, again, please accept my condolences on the death of your sister. If you happen to have any more questions, please don't hesitate to give me a call."

My initial impression of Will is he's a straight-forward, good guy. I hop back in my truck for the drive back to York. I need time to figure out my next step. I still have a nagging, raw feeling in the pit of my stomach. I know there's more to this story. The problem is, where should I go now to get my answers?

CHAPTER *fifteen*

JULIA AND LIZA
DIXON'S LAST STAND 12:00 A.M.

JULIA AND PAUL HAVE SPENT most of the night on the dance floor. This has been the first night in a long time that I am not just watching the clock. Julia has offered me a glimmer of more for my future, and I will hang on to it. I felt guilty for thinking about a happy future after just losing my dad. I miss him, and it feels surreal. He may not have shown me the best love, but he was still my dad.

"Hey, Liza. What has you so deep in thought?" Julia asks as she makes her way to the bar from the dance floor. I laugh to myself and consider the potential of her knowing all my family drama.

"I was wondering if you could tell me more about the project you mentioned," I ask.

She looks at me with excitement. "Like I told you earlier, I am a farm girl, but I graduated from college and received a degree in marketing. My goal is to help my family's farm expand. We need to create a brand. I want to use your skills in photography to help build this brand."

I am blown away. This wild girl I met a few hours ago has this whole other life. She continues filling me in on the project, and as I listen to her, I notice I have not seen Paul in the last few minutes.

"Julia, this is an amazing opportunity, and I feel lucky you are giving me this chance. It is crazy, we met a few hours ago, but I feel like we have been friends for years." I figure this is my chance to tell her how I feel before Paul wanders back. I like him, but it just feels personal between Julia and me. She smiles, adding a wink.

"I could not agree with you more, and you will get a phone call this week, don't worry," she assures me.

I want to jump for joy like a kid at Christmas. Instead, I ask about her date.

"Where did Paul go?" I serve a couple of beers to some guys a few seats down from Julia while I wait for her response.

"He had to step outside and take a call from his brother. Plus, he said it would give him a chance to check the weather before we leave. He is giving me time to decide if I am going home with him tonight. He offered me a ride on his bike and to hang with him after we leave here," she explains.

"Oh, wow! You have some big decisions to make. I know for sure what my choice would be, but this is your night," I tell her as I put another cup of water in front of her. She looks at me, and this is the first time tonight she isn't smiling. "Julia, what's wrong? Do you not want to go home with him? You don't have to do anything you don't want to," I tell her, emphasizing the "anything" part.

She reaches over and pats the top of my hand.

"Liza, you are a good friend. The problem is me. I am still hung up on the bike Paul restored for my brother, and the fact it will be delivered this week. He doesn't know this, but I had envisioned my brother inviting me to ride with him. The moment would mean he finally accepts me as more than just his little sister. We would ride on the back roads. It would be a longtime dream coming true. It's childish of me to sit here and wish for a ride with my big brother. I can have a ride tonight with an amazing man, under the night sky,"

Julia finishes, but it feels like she wants me to tell her what choice to make.

"I know you are torn between the dream ride with your brother and the kick-ass ride now with Paul. The thing I can offer you is to go with your heart. The gesture of having your brother's bike restored is the most thoughtful thing. If you feel like taking a ride with Paul tonight, then you deserve to have happiness and joy. You certainly have done plenty for your brother in my book. As far as Paul, I feel he would understand if you explain to him your feelings on the ride with your brother." I share my thoughts and truly hope it helps her decide.

LIZA

I HAVE BEEN RUNNING AROUND town today, gathering information from local dairy farms regarding their current productions. This is the information I will use in my presentation to Jackson. There are quite a few small farms here in York. It puts into perspective the size of Costello Farms, and how Julia's family has kept it thriving for years. I talked to several local farmers and learned their perception of the Costello's and their farm, in general. The great thing is that all the feedback was positive, and the family has a fantastic reputation in the area.

The perception surrounding Julia's family is that they are extremely hardworking and honest, but several farms want to top them in production and overall growth. It is important for me to incorporate these key factors into my presentation, which is why I could not sleep last night and I have been here working since before sunrise. This presentation to Jackson is important. I've done nothing like this before, so I watched several online videos to help me prepare. It is a damn good thing I am a good student. I want to nail this presentation, not for me, but for my connection to the project

Julia wanted me to work on. It makes me sad to reflect that if she were here helping me right now, I wouldn't be this anxious or worried.

Jackson hasn't decided if I am helping or hurting his family. I have my pride and want to show him I am helping. He was gone all day yesterday so I was able to relax and gather all the information needed for this presentation. It's solid. I've worked my tail off on the research, and I finally feel ready. I'm trying to finish one last read-through when I hear Jackson walk into the office. He looks freaking handsome today, with his black button-down shirt and dark jeans.

He drops his belongings down on his desk then turns and looks my way. "Are you ready to dazzle? Because I am excited to hear your ideas," he says as he sits down at his desk.

Does he really mean those words?

"I'm ready, but I'm curious if it will be only us." I am praying he asked his mom or Frankie to join us. It can't hurt to have rein-forcements.

"Mom and Frankie are coming down to listen to your presenta-tion. They will be here in a few minutes," he replies. I hear the skep-ticism in his voice, and see it on his face.

"Good deal. I'll set things up while we're waiting for them," I answer. I make my way to a large table in the center of the office. It takes me the whole ten minutes to get everything perfect. The ladies arrive, and they both appear excited about my presentation. It's nice to have some warmth in the room. Having them here helps put me at ease, much different from Jackson's arrival.

"Good morning, Liza. We're eager to hear your ideas," Maxine exclaims as she walks to the sofa and sits with Frankie. I feel a blush creep up my neck at the memory of Jackson and me on the sofa not too long ago. It is crazy that of all days, today I have to deal with his mother and grandmother sitting in the exact spot where we almost got naked. I clear those thoughts from my head and focus on this presentation as it's time to get started.

"Thank you all for coming. I understand how important your schedules are, and I don't want to waste any of your time." My nerves are jittery, and I feel this as I walk to my laptop. I take a deep breath and then push the enter key on my keyboard and begin to explain my research. "I've spent the past few days learning background information on Costello Farms and, as you know, I don't claim to have any marketing experience, but I can offer a fresh perspective." I click enter again and look at each of their faces.

"Yesterday offered me the opportunity to do a great amount of research in the area. I visited a few of your neighbors, and I can honestly say Costello Farms provides a wide variety of products to locals. Your on-site storefront operates several days a week and gives the community a variety of cheeses and fresh milk." I stop and check the pulse of the room. There is silence among my audience, but everyone appears engaged. I continue and click to my next slide.

"I think we should increase marketing and add social media blasts. We can build on sales in the storefront. Over the past two days, I also learned from neighboring local farms that they offer self-guided tours. I feel confident it would be received well here. We can select appropriate times, and base them on production schedules. We would advertise tours to help increase foot traffic at the store. The other big draw for Costello Farms would be to post videos online of Jackson and the equine therapy program through social media and our website. We can show everyone how amazing Jackson is with the horses, share details on the therapy program, and explain how it can help so many people."

I stop for a second, right before I click the last slide. I look at Jackson to see his reaction. He is keeping his poker face on. No sort of tell at all. I move to the last slide.

"The last addition for the summer will be homemade ice cream for sale in the storefront. We could employ local kids home for summer break." I click off the presentation and turn to everyone before I explain the most significant part. "The photographs I plan to take here on the farm are going to be plastered on all of our social media platforms. We'll have live media events to gain interest in happenings around the farm. An example could be a kick-off of our homemade ice cream sale and invite the community to sample the new flavors. I've thought it would be great to incorporate cheese samples while pushing milk sales in the store-front." I slow for a second to let them take in the information, but I don't stop yet. "I plan to follow Jackson around the farm over the next few days to obtain videos and photos of him working during equine sessions. I think this promotion will be huge for Costello Farms in the community." I finish and take a seat at the table to wait for feedback.

"Liza, you outdid yourself, my dear. I love all your ideas! I say yes." Frankie claps. I adore her.

"I agree with Frankie. I like your presentation and the ideas for the farm. Great job, Liza. I will be realistic and tell you it will take a lot of hard work and cooperation from everyone, but I feel we can all chip in and get it done." Maxine gives two thumbs up.

I am getting excited I might have pulled this off. "Jackson, do you have any feedback?" I ask with a high level of trepidation.

He sits there for a minute, then finally answers. "I honestly am not sure adding ice cream, free tours, and cheese samples will bring in the revenue this farm needs to keep surviving. I can say, Liza, you've done a great amount of research and hard work. It's impressive." He then stands up before walking out of the office. I am not sure how to take his exit. He didn't shoot it down, but he didn't approve it either.

I turn to Maxine and Frankie after he leaves.

"There isn't another place like this farm with these options close to town. Costello Farms will attract local families wanting a place with food and attractions, and one that won't break their budget," I insist. "The same people visiting or checking the website will see the promotion of Jackson's equine therapy."

"Liza, please don't let Jackson discourage you. We love your ideas and want to move forward with everything. Take the rest of today off. I've got to talk with Jackson's dad about this, and I will let you know how we're moving forward on everything tomorrow. Fair enough?" Maxine asks.

"You've earned a day of relaxation," Frankie agrees. She stands and hugs me.

"Thanks for everything, ladies. I couldn't have done this presentation without your support and beautiful faces," I tell them. They don't know how much their presence means to me.

"I've got my things. I'll see you tomorrow." We say goodbye to each other, and I walk to my car. Jackson isn't around anywhere. As I get in my car and start down the driveway, this makes me happy. He left me with a few things to consider. I have put a ton of hard work and hours into my presentation, and despite having never done anything of this magnitude before, I know these ideas will work.

I had a crazy dream about Julia. She was here on the farm and had joined the celebration. She attended the ribbon-cutting ceremony along with a large crowd of people and kids running all around. I know she is guiding me toward these ideas, and her brother may have reservations, but I trust my research and instincts.

I am certain my dreams are premonitions into the future of this farm. Jackson needs to give them—and me—a chance. Could Julia be guiding me through dreams to help her family? Could she be sharing things she wasn't able to finish? The possibility makes me more determined than ever to follow through.

CHAPTER
sixteen

JULIA AND LIZA
DIXON'S LAST STAND 12:30 A.M.

"Do you have our tab ready? We're leaving," Julia informs me as she stands at the bar. She had left for a bit after our talk to join Paul outside.

"Yep, I'll grab it for you." I walk to the register to print their receipt and hear Paul ask her if she is going home with him.

She looks at me with a little hesitation but then answers. "I would love to ride home with you tonight."

He nods and checks his phone. "The weather is looking clear for the rest of the night. There was a thunderstorm earlier, but the roads should be dry now." He reassures Julia with a gentle kiss.

This guy is a keeper for sure.

"I know you two will have a blast riding under the stars," I tell them, hoping to give Julia a little reassurance.

Paul sets down his phone and pulls his wallet from his back pocket. Julia grabs her wallet out of her purse at the exact moment, but he stops her by gently laying his hand over hers, whispering that he is taking care of their tab. Paul places his credit card on top of the receipt and pushes it my way.

"I got this, baby. No chance of you paying." He chuckles.

"You are way too sweet. Thanks for a wonderful time tonight," she says as she hugs him. I pick up Paul's receipt and card to process. I watch as he pulls back from Julia.

"Our night is far from over," he says, the flintiness unmistakable in his voice. I also notice a whole lot of deviousness in his smile. It suddenly gets hot in here.

"Liza, it was awesome to meet you and hang with you tonight," he says as he signs the receipt I placed in front of him.

I smile. "I feel the same way, and I look forward to seeing you in Dixon's again soon. Julia's car will be fine parked here tonight, but I have to ask, are you sure you are okay to drive this late?" I ask all my customers right before closing, but these two are now close friends.

He doesn't hesitate. "Yes, I live ten minutes up the road, and have been either riding or operating motorcycles since before I officially got my driver's license. No need to worry," he answers with confidence. Julia heads to my end of the bar and I step from behind to meet her.

"Liza, I'll call you early next week and set a time for us to meet and discuss the details of our project. I'm excited, and you're perfect for the job. Keep taking pictures," she says as she hugs me.

"Thanks for tonight. I feel lucky that our paths crossed," I respond, returning her hug. Julia laughs loudly, then pulls away and walks to Paul by the front door. He offers a wave, and then they are gone. There is something wild and wonderful that attracts people to Julia, and this potential project could be exciting.

LIZA

I TURN MY CAR AROUND and head back to the barn. I need to find Jackson and make him listen. This time I'm not leaving without one final try. This project is way too important. My presentation was solid, and the research took me days to collect. I am actually pissed off thinking about his attitude. The next thing I know, I'm past the barn and pulling up to Jackson's house. I park my car and walk up to his front door. I intend to knock on the main door, but it is open and his screen door is the only barrier.

"Jackson? Hey, it's Liza. You here?" I holler. I stand there and wait for him to respond. *Hang tough,* I tell myself. *No backing down.*

He doesn't respond or come to the door, so I try the screen and find it's unlocked. I open the door and step inside, and hear music playing toward the back of the house. I figure he might be in the kitchen. I make my way down the hallway, and pass through the living room, continuing to announce my presence.

I'm inside his home, but I still don't get an answer. Might he have company? His house is neat and orderly, but my attention is on the hardwood floors. They look like old barn wood. I love this feature, and it's something I've wished for in my own home. I'm surprised by his organization. I'm not sure why, but I imagined his house would be more unkempt.

I make my way to his kitchen and walk around. He is not in it. The space is big but still feels cozy. It reminds me of a smaller version of Maxine and Anthony's kitchen. I turn and head back down the hallway. The music is louder on the left side of the house. It must be where the bedrooms are.

Nope, I'm not going back there. I keep my eyes straight ahead and decide it's best if I leave. I'm a couple of steps from the front door when I hear footsteps behind me. I freeze in my spot.

"Why are you in my house?" Jackson asks.

I notice that the music has stopped, but honestly, I don't want to turn around. He must have just finished a shower, because I caught the fresh aroma of the body wash. He smells incredible.

"Liza, why are you standing inside my house?" he asks, but this time with more projection. I finally calm my brain enough to respond.

"I tried knocking and yelling through the door, but there wasn't an answer so I stepped inside. I want to speak with you, but maybe now is not a good time. You seem busy." I try to take a step toward the front door.

"Stop right there. You felt strongly enough to break in here a few minutes ago. I figure it is best you tell me what brought you here."

I don't know if I should run toward the door or show him I have a spine and say my peace.

"You certainly had the nerve to come storming into my house, why aren't you brave now?" he asks with a teasing tone to his voice.

"I am brave, but had second thoughts when I stepped inside and heard music coming from the hallway. Then I thought I was interrupting something," I respond, then figure running to the door is my best option.

I didn't anticipate how fast he could be. He moved quickly and blocked my way in only a dark green towel. Hell, he has no shame. The towel is hanging low on his hips, and leaves little to the imagination. He sure is glorious, with his sleeve of tattoos and chiseled chest. Then I catch the shimmer of his dog tags lying against his muscular chest. Jackson's hair is still damp from his shower. How can I talk to him when he looks like this?

"Would it bother you if I have company?" His body is still blocking my escape. I can't answer. I need to shout the word, "No!" This might persuade him to let me leave out his front door, but if I open my mouth my answer will be, "Yes."

"Is there a problem?" He looks right at me and has the sexiest grin on his face. I know deep down it is time to leave before there is no turning back. He is distracting and infuriating at the same time. I reach for the door handle one last time and try to step around him. He doesn't move at all, not one inch.

I look up and see his eyes are full of fire.

"Will you please move out of my way?" I make another huge mistake by putting my hands on his chest and attempting to push him. A jolt of electric current makes me jerk away from him. "Why won't you move?"

"I should move, but the actual movement I plan to make is with you in my arms toward my bedroom," he declares. The look of pure heat in his eyes warns me he will make good on his word. He bends close to my ear and whispers. "Liza, tell me what you want?"

I shake my head, trying to decide how I will answer, but knowing the whole time what my answer will be. My body wants this man, with a full-on fire burning in my core, and it's raging right now. It doesn't help that I've zeroed in on the water droplets from Jackson's shower dripping off his dog tags and onto his impressive chest. His broad shoulders make his chiseled muscles huge. I'm a complete goner.

I tug at Jackson's dog tags and bring his head down to my face. He wastes no time, his mouth attacking my lips. This man is my kryptonite. He lifts me and I wrap my legs around his waist. Holding me up with one arm, he uses the other to shut the front door. He keeps his mouth on mine the whole time. It feels like we only have minutes left on this earth with the way Jackson kisses me. His deep kisses leave my lips drenched in his passion, and I find myself attracted to every ounce of this man. He carries me down the hall to his bedroom and lays me down on the bed.

Jackson's king-size bed has a beautiful black iron headboard, and I hope we'll make full use of it. I grab for him, and he revisits my mouth as my hands run up and down his muscular back. I find it hard to believe his green towel still on his hips. It's one strong towel. He eases back and looks me over. His legs splayed across mine, Jackson's hands move to the top button of my jeans. His eyes lock on mine for approval. I nod with a smile, and he unbuttons my jeans and lowers my zipper. There is a noticeable rise coming from under his towel, and I want to tear it away to reveal his body.

Suddenly, I feel more confident and move my hand across the top of his green towel. I look at him, waiting for his approval as he had waited for mine. He gives it quickly with a sexy nod. I pull away his bath towel and let it fall. In his current position, I get a fantastic view of his package, and oh, how glorious it is. I reach again and stroke along his full length. I keep my rhythm steady, and Jackson tips his head back, letting a groan escape. He doesn't allow me to stroke him for long. Bending forward, he dips his tongue in my mouth and fills me with nothing less than pure heat.

While his mouth devours mine, Jackson makes quick work of removing my boots, socks, and jeans. He has also found my sexy white lace hip-hugger panties. His hands look good on me. The color of his tattoos against my skin is mind-blowing. Those same hands slip my shirt off. My matching bra is now on display, and he lets loose a low, long growl.

He kisses the top of each breast, and I like the attention he gives them. I feel his hands on my hips as he pulls my body up against his. Jackson moves his head down, leaving a trail of light kisses along my stomach and around my navel. I never imagined I would find my navel sexy, but with his mouth touching me there, it might be one of my new favorite spots.

Jackson suddenly turns me over, then growls again.

"You have the sweetest backside, and I have been dreaming about it for weeks." He cups both of my cheeks before leaning over me and kissing down my back. Jackson owns me right now. He unhooks my bra and tosses it on the floor. I arch my back, and he brings his hands around to cup my breasts.

I love his hands on my body. I stare at his artwork, and his past stories along the arm holding my body. The tattoos turn me on. My breasts fill his hands and it is sensual having his hard-working hands on my body. He rubs his length against my backside, and I feel the abundant evidence of his arousal.

Jackson flips me onto my back and brings his mouth down on mine. I feel light-headed as he slides my panties down my legs, bringing his face near the juncture of my thighs before teasing me lightly with his tongue. I get a whole-body jerk because of the electric sensation that his tongue is sending through me. He begins gently blowing every few seconds to heighten the effect. I can't take it!

"It's too much! Please, give it all to me. I need all of you," I beg. This is not my usual way, but he turns me on like a rocket. Jackson leans toward the bedside table. He opens a drawer and retrieves a condom. I watch him slip it on. He moves off the bed and stands at the end. I don't have a chance to worry for too long about what he's doing.

Jackson reaches for my legs and pulls me to the edge. I am excited to try this new position. He takes my feet and pulls them up against his chest then leans his body against them. This position spreads my thighs and opens me up for him. He enters my center slowly at first, and I adjust to how spectacular he feels. Jackson pushes deeper and drives harder into me.

I've died and gone to heaven, I think as my head swims.

We quickly find our groove, and I can't tell where my body ends and his begins. He pushes deeper still, and then I feel him pulsating right as my climax begins. His hips thrust a few more times into me in quick succession. I grab him tight to keep the sensation going. I grab his arms to pull him closer to me, but he eases away and lets my legs drop. I gasp as his body moves away from mine. He suddenly grabs my ankles and spreads my legs wide apart. I feel the weight of his body on mine, as he thrusts with one last deep dive.

Oh, my dear god!

Our bodies already fit perfectly, but this feeling tops it. Jackson leans forward and whispers low in my ear.

"You feel so good, Liza."

We grind into each other a few more times as our climaxes subside. He finally collapses beside me, and I try to slow my breathing. We both move up the bed and lean back against the pillows.

This was beyond words.

CHAPTER
seventeen

JACKSON

I'M STRUGGLING WITH THE REALITY of Liza sleeping in my bed right now. She is beautiful and I enjoy looking at her, but I find it hard to grasp that she came here to see me yesterday. She blew me away the moment I caught her standing in the middle of my living room. The first thing I asked her was why she was in my house, and she said she needed to ask a question. I never heard the question because I picked her up and kissed her. Liza has influenced me since the first time I laid eyes on her. She may not know it, but I found her beautiful face in the sea of sadness at Julia's funeral service. She was sitting near the entrance, looking around, and the minute I stepped out from the back hallway, I locked eyes with her.

There wasn't much from the day that was good, but Liza's beauty stood out, and my curiosity was immediately sparked. I didn't know who she was and how she and Julia knew each other, but I was determined to figure it out. I have been standoffish with Liza, but she has drawn me in. Julia needs to be my priority right now. I need to know what unfolded that night, but afterward, I want to explore more with Liza.

If she will give me the time.

Liza stirs, and I watch as she stretches. I could learn to like this.

"What's the time?" she asks, looking around for a clock.

"It's 5:30 am," I respond, then kiss her lips. Does she care about morning breath? Liza doesn't flinch, kissing me back and lingering there with me.

"Damn, woman. You might make me late," I tell her.

"Are you heading to the barn?" Liza asks as she pulls the covers up higher. I find her sudden modesty adorable, as these are the same parts I licked, sucked, or loved on last night. I smile at her.

"Why are you smiling?" she asks, sounding annoyed.

"I like the fact you are shy this morning. Is it because the sun is coming up?" I tease.

Liza grabs one of my pillows and launches it at me. The problem with her plan is the bed covers drop, and I get a glimpse of her magnificent breasts. They are a beautiful sight.

"Do you know you have a picture-perfect set of breasts? I do believe every woman in town should be jealous." I laugh but get another pillow upside my head.

"It must be time for you to leave. I need to get my clothes and head to work as well," she tells me, but now she seems bothered.

"I am teasing, but accurate on your breasts. Are you okay?" I ask.

She eyes me nervously. "I would prefer not to run into your family as I leave this morning. Is there any chance one of them might stop by here or be close by?" she asks as she bounces off my bed. She grabs her clothes and hurries to the bathroom.

"I won't lie, there's always a chance of someone driving down the road in front of my house since we do things around the farm early. But I doubt anyone will knock on my door," I answer, trying to put her mind at ease. She left the bathroom door ajar, and I watch as she dresses and combs her fingers through her hair. I'm a little sad to part ways with her this morning. I know we both have work today and I worry we will probably never be intimate again. It leaves me feeling lonely.

Liza steps from the bathroom. She makes the "morning after" look fantastic. I want to kiss her again, but she looks anxious, and I get the impression that it wouldn't be a good idea right now.

"I want to talk for a few minutes before we leave," she says, and I can see the worry on her face. I understand the full-body anxiety now.

"Okay. What's on your mind?" I decide this might be best handled sitting down. I settle myself on the edge of my bed. She is leaning in the bathroom doorway.

"I came by yesterday with the intention of convincing you to support my presentation. I wanted to discuss the benefits, and show you my ideas can work for your family's farm. I know we got off track, but I'm not wrong and I wish you could understand. Please don't let this interfere with the incredible things I believe will happen." She moves closer to me while speaking, but not all the way.

"I have a reluctance, but I'm willing to give it a chance if my parents agree." I figure it is worth a shot. Liza takes the last few steps toward me.

"Thank you for trying and for giving me a chance," she says right before she kisses me. I feel her lips on mine again, and I kiss her back. I spread my legs wide so she can walk in between and allow us to be closer. Liza wraps her arms around the back of my head and cradles me. The feeling is bliss, and something I haven't experienced in a long time, if ever. I know at this moment I want this closeness again, and all that we shared last night. I want more. I crave more of Liza.

"We need to get our day started," I finally say, anxious to get going before someone shows up on my doorstep.

She looks down at me and breaks contact.

"Yes, I guess you are right," she agrees. "I need to head to my apartment and change. I will see you later this morning. I plan on getting some great shots of you with the horses during therapy," she tells me, and I can't miss the excitement in her voice. I nod as I give her one last kiss on our way from my bedroom to the front door. We both make our way to our vehicles and say our goodbyes, for now. I've never had this big of a smile on my face, and I know Julia is looking down on me laughing and saying, "I told you so."

CHAPTER
eighteen

LIZA

THE LAST TWO WEEKS HAVE been a blur. Mr. and Mrs. Costello agreed to the suggestions I made in my presentation and everyone got started right away. I've been working alongside Jackson, taking videos and photos of his sessions in the equine therapy program. It's astonishing how each student learns during their session. He manages each one differently and structures them in such a personalized nature by each student's skill level or therapy requirement. I observe as Jackson works with younger children on the autism spectrum, and those who have different physical disabilities. On top of that, he also works with adults dealing with Post Traumatic Stress Disorder, some from military service, and a few others from tragic life events.

I convinced Jackson to do a video interview with me about how he got into equine therapy. It covers his time in the military and working with his service animal Maverick. To be honest, it took all I had not to cry from the emotional stories he shares. I can tell he loved his dog greatly. Jackson's interview was candid and from the heart. The training he received in the military helped him realize he didn't want to re-enlist, wanting instead to work with service animals. He also told me stories about growing up around horses and livestock on the farm. He talked about his time down in Charlotte, North Carolina at school and then about his transition to equine therapy. The interview is inspiring. I know it will be fantastic footage for the Costello Farms website and social media sites. He is easy on the eyes, but his voice makes you want to hit repeat on the video.

Anthony and Maxine have been working on the new storefront items and the hiring of summer staff. I haven't just been working directly with Jackson; I've also been updating social media sites with photographs from the farm. Frankie manages the homemade ice cream project and is doing a great job. The new flavors are fantastic, and with support from Maxine, she has the storefront updates looking phenomenal. I know the farm ideas are a huge undertaking, and asking everyone to get it all done by the beginning of summer was a monumental task. It looks like we just might make it all happen.

The ribbon-cutting ceremony was tough to get Anthony to approve, but Maxine finally wore him down. I plan to have lots of pictures on display, and maybe a few for sale.

I'm running back to Berkeley Springs today because I need to get a special picture developed of Julia and I don't want to risk anyone in York seeing it. Dixon had called and left me a message last week about picking up my last paycheck. I figured while I'm in town it would be great to see him and grab that check.

The drive to Berkeley Springs is quiet and peaceful. I get to listen to new tunes and clear my mind for a few hours. I've been extremely busy with the events at Costello Farms and have had little time alone with my thoughts. I'm excited to see Dixon, but it also pulls me back to the night with Julia. I wonder sometimes if she is proud of our progress at the farm. I don't, however, believe she would be proud of the fact that I slept with her brother.

I walk into Dixon's and head straight for the bar, finding him leaning on the kitchen-side counter with his back to me.

"Do you know if the owner is hiring?" I ask, then start to laugh. He turns when he hears my voice and his face quickly fills with a smile.

"Liza! How the hell have you been, girl?"

I sure have missed this big guy. He comes to me and pulls me off the ground into one of his famous bear hugs. I miss these hugs and hang on for dear life. He smells spectacular, like burgers and fries. I love it.

He lets me go, and I slide down onto my feet. Dixon waves a new server over to cover the bar. He motions toward an empty table in the corner, then pulls a chair out and allows me to sit first. Such a gentleman. He may have a gruff exterior, but there is nothing but a soft heart inside.

"How are you doing?" he asks, looking concerned.

I sit for a few seconds, unsure of how to answer him. I would have given him a different answer two weeks ago, but now things seem a bit brighter.

"It feels like things are finally on track for me now. I feel better about my future," I answer, but I don't get the feeling he believes me.

"I was worried. You left town in such a hurry," he says.

I still feel bad for the way I left.

"I couldn't stay after the accident. It was too much for my heart, Dixon." I place my hand on my chest, and he nods his head in understanding.

"I left you a message a few days ago because this guy came in asking questions. He wants to talk with you."

"Who was it?" I ask, even though I already know the answer. "What did he ask or say?" I feel the panic rising.

"The brother of the girl on the motorcycle. He said he has a few questions about his sister's accident," Dixon explains.

Jackson was here and asking about me.

"You didn't tell him my name, did you?" I ask, unable to hide the dread in my voice.

Dixon looks at me, worried. "I did no such thing and you know better than to believe for a second I would. I told him to give me his name and number, and I would pass it on to you," he responds, and I feel bad for doubting him.

He pulls his wallet from his jeans pocket, takes out a business card, and hands it to me. The card is from Costello Farms and has Jackson's contact information on it. "He asked me to pass this along. He wants to talk with you."

Jackson drove here looking for answers, but thanks to Dixon's loyalty, he kept my secret. I try not to cry.

"Liza, my wish for you is to find peace. It wasn't your fault. Please stop carrying this heavy burden on your shoulders." He reaches over and squeezes my hand. I can't stop myself from crying now.

"I shouldn't have encouraged Julia to ride on Paul's bike. It wasn't my place. Why didn't I try harder to stop them from leaving?" I ask.

"It was a terrible accident. The old man was sick, and it wasn't anything you could have known. One day, you must release yourself from this." Dixon passes a napkin to me. I take it and dab each eye, then look down at Jackson's business card.

He is close to finding out the truth. It's time for me to tell them all about Julia, but I don't want it to ruin all the hard work and planning the family and farm employees have done. This event is vital to the growth of the farm. I will leave town after I tell them. My world is crashing down.

I shove Jackson's business card in my pocket and stand up. "Thank you again for taking care of me. I can never repay you." I want him to know how much his kindness means. Dixon stands and gives me another hug, a little gentler this time.

"Let me grab your last check." We both walk back to the bar to retrieve it. "Please take care of yourself and remember, I always have your back."

I smile and reach for his hand and hold on. My life will soon change, and I know I can't hide my relationship with Julia from her family much longer.

"Bye, Dixon," I say with one more smile. "I'll talk to you soon."

I drive two hours back to York with heaviness in my chest, knowing I have a limited window to speak to Jackson. He is closing in on the truth. I just hope I can hang on until after the ribbon-cutting ceremony. Julia is guiding me along on this whole project, and I want to see it finished.

I need to do this for her.

I make it back to my apartment with the hope that Ruby's would still be open, but I am not so lucky. She is closed. There goes the apple pie I'd been craving the whole drive back. I get out of my car and head toward the stairway leading to my apartment.

As I reach the stairs, I see Jackson at the bottom, leaning against the wall. Why is he standing there?

"Why are you at my door?" I ask.

He pushes himself off the wall, and I notice he has a Ruby's container in his hand. He must've eaten here tonight.

"I stopped by to see you. When you didn't answer, I went to Ruby's and grabbed dinner." He holds up his container. "How was your day?" he asks.

I blush when I lock my eyes on his leftovers, hardly listening to his words. I am starving. He hands it to me.

"You saved a life," I reply, happily taking the container from his hands. "I was busy today and didn't eat. Ran a ton of errands for the ribbon-cutting ceremony." I fill him in on my day as I unlock my door. He stands waiting behind me.

"Do you want to come upstairs? We can talk while I eat your leftovers." I giggle. He rolls his eyes at me but follows me inside.

I tell him to make himself at home while I fix my dinner, which I find is not leftovers but apple pie. Two slices, actually. I look at Jackson, and find him failing to look innocent.

"I've got coffee to go with these two slices of apple pie if you would like, and I might have some ice cream." I bought some with the temptation of Ruby's famous pie just downstairs.

"I'm good with both," Jackson replies.

My errands are the topic of conversation as I prepare our pie and coffee. He is sitting at my little dinette set that was part of

Ruby's furnishings. The set has a dark-stained circular wooden table with two matching chairs. It's plenty for me, and I find it cozy when I drink my morning cup of coffee.

"Okay, enough about my day. What brings you here?" I ask. I'm nervous around him after my visit with Dixon.

"I have two reasons for stopping by. First, my mom said you have several pictures ready for the ceremony and you need them brought to the farm. I told her I would be happy to stop by and pick them up."

Jackson doesn't continue with reason number two, taking a bit of his apple pie instead.

"That's great. I can use the help. But what's the other reason?" He gets up and takes his dishes to the sink. I wait. He suddenly looks nervous.

"I enjoyed being with you the other night, and I can't stop wishing for another night with you, Liza."

He catches me off-guard with the truth. Jackson Costello is standing in my little kitchen, leaning against my counter, telling me he wants to be with me again.

"So, the second reason for stopping by is that you enjoyed the sex?"

I had to do a gut-check. It isn't him, and this is entirely my fault. He is so far out of my league and I just can't be with him because of my tie to Julia. The relationship he doesn't know anything about.

"I'm a big girl. I don't expect you to fall in love with me after one night of sex." I hate the way I sound and the words I speak.

"That's not what I'm saying at all. I agree the sex was outstanding, but you need to know there is more to me than one night and a hot time. Please, you are way off base," Jackson tries to explain.

"This isn't going to work." I stand up. "Please lock the door when you leave." I cut him off before he can say anything else. I head toward my bedroom and I'm glad it's not a far walk from the kitchen. "Goodnight Jackson," I say as I shut the door. It's quiet for a few minutes, then I hear him in the kitchen cleaning up my dishes.

Damn. Now I feel like an asshole.

I hate all of this. The ceremony is in two days and then I can tell Julia's family everything. After that, I'll leave York.

CHAPTER
nineteen

JACKSON

THINGS DIDN'T GO THE WAY I planned. Julia completely misunderstood why I stopped by.

Damned if you do, and damned if you don't, I think as I clean up the plates left on the table. I hope it will help since she is upset with me. I honestly feel like it's more than our one night that has upset her. I can relate to flying off the handle a time or two since dealing with the loss of Julia, and think maybe this could be related to my sister. They had a friendship, and I wish Liza would share the details. I want to know more. Who knows, she might have had second thoughts since I'm Julia's brother.

I clean the rest of our mess and open the dishwasher to load our dirty dishes. It's filled with clean ones. I guess it can't hurt to help a girl out. I should leave, but I feel bad about how things went south. I quickly start to empty her dishwasher and finish up. A plate falls to the floor as I am pulling the dishes from the dishwasher. I turn to pick it up and a white piece of paper lying on the floor in front of her sink catches my eye.

I pick it up and realize it's a business card. It's my business card. Why is my card on her floor?

I turn it and see my handwriting on the back, with my cell phone number. I believe this is one of the cards I left in Berkeley Springs. It was supposed to be passed on to the bartender who served Julia the night she died or to Paul's brother.

Why does Liza have this card? My heart pounds in my chest. Should I go into the bedroom and ask her? Does she know the bartender? Does she know anything about the night Julia died? I shove the card into my jeans pocket before grabbing the pictures I promised to take back to the farm. My walk to the door is silent. There are way too many thoughts swirling around in my mind. I'm consumed with how Liza might play into all of this.

Why would she not tell me if she had information about that night? There are some big decisions to be made, and the biggest one is whether I ask her about this card before or after the ceremony. The farm needs exposure, and everyone has worked hard to make it all happen, including Liza. I want answers but I fear what they might be.

CHAPTER

twenty

JULIA AND LIZA
DIXON'S LAST STAND 1:00 A.M.

I HAVE AN HOUR UNTIL I can leave, and people are starting to close out their tabs. I enjoyed spending time with Julia and Paul. It made the night go by faster than usual. I have big decisions to make, and now they don't seem as daunting. Julia's call this coming week will give me a life outside of this bar—no offense to Dixon, who has been wonderful to me. My dreams of something more finally feel obtainable.

I'm cleaning around the bar top and picking up empty glasses when I see Dixon walking in through the front door. It's unusual for him to be here this late. For the most part, he takes the early shift.

"Hey, Dixon. Why are you back this late?" I ask as he walks to me. As he gets closer, I can see he is upset.

"There's been an accident. Two of our patrons from tonight," he explains with a look of absolute dread on his face. My stomach drops.

"What happened?" I ask, wanting and not wanting to know.

"It was a motorcycle accident, not far up the road. I got a call ten minutes ago. They're still working the scene. The police will be here soon to ask questions."

I close my eyes and tell myself it wasn't them. I need to ask him if he knows who was in the accident. Oh, my God. It can't be. Please don't let it be them.

"Liza, do you remember a young couple leaving here about an hour ago?" Dixon asks. I am frozen with fear and no words come out. I drop to my knees as the reality hits me that it really was Paul and Julia.

"Are you okay?" he asks, coming around the bar and kneeling next to me. "Did you talk to them before they left?"

I'm crying because I let them leave. Suddenly Dixon stands up and welcomes several police officers. They head back to Dixon's office to talk. My legs feel like lead. No matter how I try, I can't move them. I don't have the energy to stand up. I hear folks in the bar talking about the accident and I try to tune their voices out. One of the other bartenders tells the remaining people in the bar that we are closing early and to settle up. My heart and head hurt, and the tears won't stop pouring. It feels like forever as I wait on the floor for Dixon to come from his office with news of Julia and Paul.

"Liza, are you able to stand? The officers need to speak with you."

I look at him and nod, despite not wanting to. He helps me up, and we walk to a table and sit. It was one of the worst nights in my life. Next to the day my mom left or the night my dad died; this was right up there.

"The couple left here on a motorcycle and were involved in an accident," an officer explains to me. My vision is too blurred from tears to focus on him, and my mind is so filled with heartbreak that I can barely register anything he is saying. "It appears a truck pulled in front of them, and the driver of the truck died at the scene along with the man on the bike." My heart breaks in my chest as I listen. "The female on the bike was transported to the hospital, and they have notified her family."

"Is she okay?" I ask, fighting the lump in my throat.

"We don't have a current update on her condition," he responds.

"We need to know how much they drank, when they started, and when they stopped."

"Paul had nothing but water and soda," I reply firmly. "And Julia had a few, but she stopped a few hours before leaving. She only drank water for the rest of the night."

After they finish questioning me, they tell me they will call if they have any other questions. I sit there in disbelief. In the last moments I spent with Julia, I urged her to go for a ride on Paul's bike. I tried to help by reassuring her it would be okay. Now, she may not make it through the night.

"This is entirely my fault," I say as I turn to Dixon. "I told her it was romantic to ride under the stars." I feel the walls closing in on me and I decide I can't be in this bar anymore. "This is my last night. I can't work here. I am sorry to do this to you." I take off my apron and lay it on the bar.

"Liza, please don't quit. Take some personal time, and your job will be here when you're ready to come back," Dixon says. I feel selfish because all night I was thinking about Julia's call to me about her project.

Now she is fighting for her life, and her family is finding out their daughter has been in an accident. I imagine they are rushing to the hospital to be by her side, and Paul's family is just learning he died. This is overwhelming, because in the last four hours I was happy and laughing with them.

"Thanks for being with me. I asked Paul if he was okay to drive this late at night. He assured me he was fine." I am crying again. He stands up and puts his arms around me.

"There was no predicting that someone would pull out in front of them. This is not your fault," Dixon emphasizes.

I shrug out of his hug. "You've been like a father to me, and I can't thank you enough for helping me, but the pain right now is unbearable. I simply can't be here anymore," I tell him.

"Please know that you can always come home," he reassures me.

I turn away and leave Dixon's Last Stand.

LIZA

COSTELLO FARMS IS PACKED, AND I'm amazed that we pulled it off. The ribbon-cutting ceremony is starting. It is the last event of the day and we have about ten minutes until showtime.

"Frankie, the amount of people in attendance is incredible. There has been a steady stream of customers in the storefront all day. I hear the homemade ice cream is a big hit with parents and kids alike," I tell her with joy and surprise in my voice.

"Oh, Liza! I always had confidence you would pull off a show-stopper, and today is a huge success. It's spectacular. I love all the photographs you have on display. I keep hearing good things as people pass by," she replies. I see a twinkle in her eyes. Tonight seems magical for everyone. I look past Frankie and spot Maxine and Anthony walking this way.

"Hello, ladies. It looks like things are going great here at the storefront. We checked the equine therapy demonstration, and Jackson had the crowd involved and enchanted. We will get a bunch of inquiries for sure. He told us he would be over in a few minutes. I'm impressed by all the folks from the town here to support Costello Farms," Anthony states with pride.

"Hey, everyone. Let's get this show started." I turn around, and Jackson is standing there. He looks handsome but irritated. I smile at him, but he doesn't look my way. I find it a bit strange. We didn't end on good terms the other night, but I had assumed we could be cordial for this event. I guess he doesn't feel the same.

"We would like for you to represent Costello Farms tonight and have Liza by your side," Maxine says. "She can cut the official ribbon after your speech. You both have worked hard these past two weeks to make all of this happen. Please accept our appreciation, and we want you both to know Julia would be proud," Maxine says through her tears. Jackson walks to his mom and hugs her, then shakes his dad's hand. He kisses his grandmother on her cheek. This intimate gesture must be their thing. He doesn't acknowledge me at all.

He turns and walks toward the stage. I give everyone an awkward smile before following him up there. We had built a small stage in front of the storefront for the ceremony. This day signifies the kickoff for all the changes at Costello Farms.

"Are you all right?" I ask as we walk up on stage, but he doesn't respond.

What in the world is wrong?

This day is a happy occasion, and a chance to celebrate his family's farm, not to mention the big goals Julia wanted them all to achieve.

He starts his speech by welcoming everyone and describing the significance of the day. He shares about his family and their farm's history, explains how they are looking forward to continued involvement with the town. Jackson sounds professional and proud of the farm, and he looks damn good in his outfit. He is wearing black pants and a dark blue dress shirt. My thoughts drift to how sexy he would look if he rolled up those long sleeves to reveal his tattoos and muscular forearms. I am staring hard at him while he is talking to the crowd. I can see a hint of sadness in his eyes.

This would be too much of a reminder that Julia should be here standing on stage with him instead of me.

When he is finished talking, he walks to me and passes the scissors. I'm nervous as the crowd watches me cut the ribbon. Jackson steps back and lets me move up to perform my task. I pull the ribbon up and snip it, and the crowd cheers. I'm proud I was able to help the Costello's, and in the process, feel like I helped Julia.

There is a sudden movement and Jackson puts his hand on my lower back. I turn my head to look at him. He eases me toward the stairs, gesturing for me to head off the stage.

"Is everything ok?" I ask, I step onto the ground from the bottom step. He is near me, and we turn to stare at each other. Jackson picks up my right hand and then places something in my palm. It feels like paper. I look down to see exactly what it is, and my heart sinks.

It's Jackson's business card, the one Dixon gave me the other day. I don't know how he found it, but it doesn't matter at this point.

"We need to talk in private, wouldn't you agree?" Jackson asks.

My head tries to signal my mouth to shout back some smartass answer, then walk away from him, but my heart is telling me it is time to come clean. I nod in agreement. He grabs my hand that is holding his business card and pulls me through the crowd. The craziest part for me is the fact that I still get the same electric jolt the moment our skin makes contact. This is bittersweet.

He opens the passenger door to his truck and waits until I climb in, then walks around to his side. Jackson starts his truck and drives in silence. It's strange because I want to reach over and touch him, to feel his skin, maybe for the last time.

We arrive at his house, and I don't move. After Jackson turns off the engine, he takes a deep breath and climbs out his truck. He makes his way to my side of the truck, and I notice his manners are not gone just because he is mad at me. Jackson opens my door for me and I get out then follow him to his front door. He opens the door and waits for me to walk inside. I move forward into the living room, but I am afraid to turn around. I don't want to face him. I know the day is here to tell him everything, but it also means I lose him forever. Jackson is still mad, and I can hear his heavy breathing just behind me.

He makes his way around to stand in front of me. I close my eyes for a moment, knowing the questions are coming. I open them to see his dark eyes staring at me, and his chest is rising and falling at a frantic pace. My arms ache to reach around him and bring his chest against mine and hold the embrace all night.

Would he let me?

I don't answer the question in my head before his mouth is on mine. The kiss is gentle, a whisper on my mouth. This was not like the kiss in his living room after he caught me trespassing in his house. That kiss was meant to devour, and somehow this kiss feels more formidable.

Jackson releases me and steps away. He seems to be trying to clear his head and it gives me the courage to speak.

"Why did you kiss me?" I ask.

He holds my gaze and replies without hesitation. "I wanted to taste your lips one last time because I have a feeling that after we talk, it will never happen again." He heads to the sofa and sits down.

My legs are suddenly unsteady, but I make my way anyway and sit in the overstuffed chair across from the sofa. We look at each other for a few seconds before Jackson breaks the silence.

"Liza, please tell me how you ended up with my business card."

Here starts the crumbling of my life at Costello Farms. I begin to tell him the details of my friendship with his sister.

"I had been working at Dixon's Last Stand as a bartender until the night Julia died. Dixon gave me your card when I went to pick up my last paycheck. He said you had been in and wanted to speak with the bartender who served Julia. I planned to tell you and your family after the ribbon-cutting ceremony," I explain and wipe away a falling tear.

He eases closer to the edge of the sofa and continues with more questions. "Tell me the whole truth. Were you with Julia the night she died? Did you serve her and Paul?" Jackson asks.

I exhale and speak. "I worked the night of Julia's accident, yes. I met Julia, and we became fast friends. It's hard to explain, but it feels like destiny had a hand in our path crossing."

He looks like he doesn't understand anything I'm saying. "Did this destiny include you serving them alcohol and letting them ride away in the middle of the night on a motorcycle?" He had an accusing tone in his voice.

"I served Julia two drinks, but Paul was completely sober. He only drank soda. I asked them before they left if they were both good to leave. They assured me they didn't have far to go, and Paul was sober. He also was an experienced rider," I respond, but I couldn't keep my voice from rising.

"You spent time in my home. My family shared intimate details of her life with you, and at no time did you say a word about this to any of us." His voice grows louder. "How could you treat us like fools?" he asks, a coldness filling his dark eyes.

It's impossible to convince him of my friendship with his sister.

"Jackson, I care deeply for you and your family," I tell him. He doesn't respond right away, instead running his hands through his hair. He seems to be gathering his thoughts.

"Why hide your relationship with Julia if you did nothing wrong?" he asks as he gets up from the couch. "Why not tell us right away if you are innocent?"

"I was sad and scared. I only planned to attend Julia's funeral. Frankie invited me to come to the farm after the funeral and, to be honest, I wanted to learn more about Julia," I explain. "I spent four hours getting to know your sister, and we hit it off. Julia said she would call me the next week to work on a photography project."

He looks at me from where he is standing, then moves toward the front window, looking out on the farm. "Julia sent me a text saying that she met someone who could help us with photography," Jackson admits before shaking his head. "This is too overwhelming. I wish you had said something the moment you arrived." He turns around from the window and faces me again.

He stands there for a minute, as if he is trying to figure out the connections between everything.

"I'm sorry. I walked into the bar that night broken-hearted. My photography was a dream I kept hidden until Julia snooped and found a few pictures on my phone. She made me an offer. She was a friend when I needed one. I owed her, and wanted to pay my respects. I didn't plan on getting involved with your family, that happened by chance. Frankie has a way of drawing people in." To my surprise, he nods in agreement.

"I held you during the storm while your body was shaking. I deserved to know the truth." He hands me his truck keys. "You can take my truck back to the main house. Liza, I'm sorry from the

bottom of my heart, and genuinely wish you could've trusted me."
Jackson releases a deep breath full of frustration and turns away
from me. He walks down the hall towards his bedroom. I hear the
echo come back up the hallway as he closes his door. The sting feels
familiar. I stand in his living room for a minute and wish like hell I
had the nerve to go to him and beg for forgiveness.

CHAPTER twenty-one

LIZA

I DECIDE TO DRIVE LATE into the night after leaving Jackson's and head back to Berkeley Springs since I have nowhere else to go. I'm broken and ashamed. Dixon is my only family now. My mind keeps replaying all of my stupid choices, from the day I arrived in York for Julia's funeral until yesterday. Dixon said I can always come back, and I know he won't judge me. I'm exhausted when I pull into the parking lot, just as the sun is coming up. I figure Dixon should be here in a little less than an hour, and a nap sounds good while I wait for him to arrive.

A knock on my window wakes me from my nap. I find Dixon is standing outside my car, so I roll my window down to greet him.

"I didn't figure I would see you again this soon, and definitely not this early in the morning." He looks in my car as he waits for my reply. I don't have the heart to sugarcoat anything.

"Jackson found out the truth about me working here. He found the business card you gave me the other day and he confronted me last night with it," I blurt. Dixon opens my car door and ushers me out.

"Let's go inside and get some coffee started. It may be a long morning for both of us." He helps me get out of the car and I lock it before following him inside.

"Do you know what you will do now?" he asks as the coffee brews.

"I'm not sure. I have fallen for the whole family, and I secretly wish they could be mine." I am not embarrassed by this truth. "It certainly wasn't my intention to have feelings for anyone, or to go to York and withhold information."

Dixon makes his way around the bar to the table I am sitting at and pulls up a chair. He puts a box of tissues on the table between us, and I feel the tears start to fall. Knowing tears are streaming down my face doesn't bother me. I am numb inside. I grab a couple tissues to wipe my face.

I feel him looking at me with sympathy and compassion.

"Honey, I know you are probably running it over in your mind, how it all went wrong. You got close with the whole family. And, please, try not to forget that it is okay to love people. We can't answer the big question like why Julia died. I am a believer in a higher power for that answer," Dixon shares. He always had faith. "You're not a bad person. You did nothing wrong except for withholding important details about the relationship between you and Julia." Dixon doesn't hold back. I know he is right, but I still have a hard time thinking I didn't play a part in Julia's death. He puts his hand on top of mine.

"I apologized and tried to explain my connection with his sister, but Jackson didn't understand," I told Dixon. He pulls his hands away from mine as he stands.

"Our coffee is finally ready," he says before disappearing to the kitchen. After a minute, he comes back with two hot cups in his hands. It thrills me to see them.

"You need to give Jackson time to forgive you, and to heal. Remember that he lost his sister. He hasn't come to grips with his world being blown apart, and now he has been thrown for a loop with this new information." Dixon is good at helping me see the roller coaster of emotions Jackson could be feeling right now. I sip my coffee as he continues. "Please give him time, and I think you both will find your way back to each other." He picks up his mug and takes a drink. The sun is shining bright through the bar windows now. It's shaping up to be a beautiful morning.

"You win, Dixon. It makes sense to me, and I think I see the steps I need to take. I'll give Jackson time to heal from Julia's death, and hopefully one day he can forgive me. One day, he'll see I never intended to hurt him or his family." I smile at Dixon, and he nods back at me. "I can move forward knowing in my heart I helped them. My intentions were good, I just made the wrong choice when I didn't tell them about my connection to Julia from the beginning." I feel better than I did during my drive here this morning.

"Liza, you will find the peace you deserve. Let me fix you break-fast." Dixon makes his way to the kitchen. He wasn't giving me the chance to argue, and to be honest, I was hungry.

"That sounds great. Thanks again for taking care of me." Dixon always made me feel safe and gave me the best advice. He fixes breakfast pretty quickly, and then we eat together. It gives us time to talk about other life events. I fill him in on how my ideas and the ceremony went at the farm. He told me he was proud and he never had a doubt I would do a great job. After we finish breakfast, I decide it's time for me to head back.

"Dixon, I don't know how to thank you for everything you do and your continued support." I wrap him in a big hug.

"I am glad I can be here when you need me," Dixon whispers as he returns my hug.

The drive back to York doesn't feel long. My brain is occupied with ideas on how I can give Jackson time to forgive me and space to heal. It will be easier for us both to do this since I've decided to leave town. My direction is undetermined as of now, but I feel sure I can find my way. I stop into Ruby's before going upstairs to pack. She needs to know that I will no longer need the apartment. The diner is busy with the lunch rush. I go to the counter and ask if she is available. They tell me she will see me in a few minutes, so I sit down at the counter and wait. I turn when I hear the front door open and watch as Frankie walks in.

Just my luck.

Frankie spots me immediately and waves me to her booth.

"It's great to see you," she says with a grin.

"Hello, Frankie. How are you doing?" I ask, looking around.

"I'm waiting for my friend Lois to join me. I'm early. Please sit until she arrives."

I oblige and sit at her table.

"I had a long talk with Jackson this morning," she says, surprising me. "How are you doing?"

"I am tired, but I'm doing all right. I am sorry, Frankie. I should have told you the moment we first met."

"I forgive you, Liza. You have your reasons, and I am a true believer in second chances. I would love to hear more about how you met Julia." She pulls our hands together and I give in, telling her the full details from that night. The story about Julia and Paul, and how we became fast friends. She listens to my story, then asks me a big question I wasn't prepared for.

"How do you truly feel about Jackson?"

I am speechless. How do I feel?

"How is he this morning?" I ask without answering her question.

"He is upset and confused. Jackson has feelings for you, Liza. My gut is telling me you have feelings for him too. Am I correct?" She won't let it go.

I believed at first it was lust, but soon it turned into much more. I'm not sure how to tell Frankie.

"I do have feelings for Jackson, but when I am ready, I'll share that with him. My first priority is to settle a few personal matters, and then I'm leaving town," I declare. It felt good to be completely honest with her.

"Oh, Liza, please don't leave. I am not mad, and I know Jackson will forgive you. Please give him a little more time," she pleads with me, and it breaks my heart.

"I am grateful to you for all of your kindness. Julia led me to all of you and the farm." I smile and gently squeeze her hand. "I need to stand on my own for once," I say with pride.

I hear the bell ring indicating someone has entered, and look up to see her friend Lois walking in. That is perfect timing. Frankie has special powers though, because she is making it hard to leave her.

"Have a great lunch, ladies. Frankie, I will talk to you soon." I walk to the door and turn the corner to head upstairs to my apartment. It's time to handle a few loose ends.

CHAPTER *twenty-two*

JACKSON

THE PAST WEEK HAS BEEN hell, and I spent it handling all the new changes here on the farm. The therapy program has been an attraction for visitors along with the storefront. We have been slammed since the ribbon-cutting ceremony and it has been a much-needed distraction. Mom and Dad invited me for Sunday dinner, and I'm happy for a night off. I just wish they would let things rest with the conversation around Liza. It has been a week since the revelation and our fight. It was a kick in the gut to learn she was the bartender who was working the night Julia died. I know Frankie will be at dinner tonight, and she never lets things rest.

My mind wouldn't let memories of Liza fade. She is still in my heart. I have such a desire to drive to her apartment and knock on her door, but I am not sure what to say at this point. There are moments I am still furious at her for not telling me everything from the minute we met. Other times, I feel like I can forgive her. I miss her beautiful face, and I want to hold her in my arms again, if only one last time. This week was way harder than I imagined it could be. I want to honor my sister's memory, and I'm not sure if she would be okay with Liza and me being a couple. I wish I could ask her.

There is whispering as I enter the house, and I find everyone gathered around the dining room table looking at Mom's laptop.

"What are you guys doing?" I ask. My family shifts their focus to me and it makes me uncomfortable.

"Liza sent us a video file to watch and says it's a follow-up to the project from here on the farm," Mom explains before starting the video.

I try to focus on the screen, but my heart is beating fast as the music starts and I hear Julia's favorite song playing. The images appearing on-screen are of the farm. These must be the photographs that Liza took. There are so many of the main house, the barns, and more. The music fades and a video plays of me explaining the therapy program and talking about working with the horses. I forgot Liza made me do this interview.

The video finishes and Julia's song comes back on with more pictures of all of us in the family and the staff who work here. There are many stunning photos from our farm, including Julia's favorite spot. There is no doubt that Liza is talented. She definitely captured the feeling of our family.

Julia's song ends with a picture of our driveway leading away from the farm. It's a still shot featuring one of many amazing sunsets we are blessed to get here. I like her artistic touch. The music fades in again and a single image slowly forms on the screen. Script begins rolling along the bottom of the screen, and the image finally materializes. I have to blink several times to keep the tears from pouring.

Julia Costello and Paul Simmons
Forever in our hearts
Photo were taken at Dixon's Last Stand

The image is of Paul and Julia dancing, and it shows two people clearly in love. The video was already moving, and then she shares this final picture of Julia. It gives us peace to know she was happy right before the accident. I'm wiping tears off my face as I hear Liza's voice. She appears on the screen sitting on a barstool at Dixon's bar. She looks magnificent with her hair cascading around her shoulders, and her amber eyes are bright. She is attempting a smile as she looks at the camera, her nerves are obvious as she speaks.

"HELLO, EVERYONE. THIS VIDEO IS MY GIFT TO YOU. I PRAY THE image brings a little peace to knowing Julia was happy in her last hours. I forgot I had this image on my cell phone of her and Paul dancing that night.

"I found a connection to Julia and to all of you during the time I spent at Costello Farms. Please know I am sorry for not telling you immediately that I had met Julia the night she died. I feared how you would view me. I made a bad choice in withholding the information. I will always regret that decision.

"I feel you should know a little background on me, and not for sympathy, but because you deserve to know. I didn't have a real family growing up. Dad tried the best he could to provide me with stability, but it wasn't a warm or loving home. When I met Frankie at the church service, it was instant warmth. She invited me to the farm, and it almost seems Julia wanted me to meet all of you and see the place where she grew up. She walked into Dixon's that night and we hit it off. I guess you can't fight a force of nature, she was wild to my timid.

"For most of my life, I took care of my dad and never had a chance to live my dreams. I'm not complaining. I was his daughter and wouldn't have done it any other way, but Julia offered me a chance for a new beginning after his death.

"Please know that you will all be in my heart forever. Take care of each other."

. . .

As THE SCREEN WENT BLACK, I WAS CRUSHED BY THE NEED FOR fresh air. Frankie grabs my hand as I try to pass by her. "Where are you going?"

I don't reply. I pull out of her grasp and walk out the front door to stand on the porch. It takes me a minute to catch my breath. I close my eyes and run through all the images from the video. Liza is leaving, and it is my fault. I blew up at her and I'm mad at myself. I need to find her and apologize.

Frankie walks outside.

"I can't talk right now. Please respect my wishes," I ask her as I sit on the top step.

"I won't ask you to talk, but I do need a quick favor," she says. I look at her in frustration. "I left my cane in the barn. My hip is acting up today and I need it," she tells me. She hasn't used it in a few weeks, but I know I can't say refuse and leave my grandmother without her cane.

"Fine, but after I get back, I'm heading to town," I tell her and walk toward the barn. I relish in a few moments alone to gather my feelings about Liza. Maybe she will give me a chance to talk with her. I know I don't deserve it, but I want to apologize. She never shared about her dad. I had no idea he died recently, and realize the grief she must have been going through all on her own.

As I reach the barn and walk through the door, my phone dings with a new message. I pull my phone from my jeans pocket to see who sent me a message really quick before I look for the cane. I'm shocked to see it's from Liza.

Liza: *Jackson, this was planned to be delivered the week Julia died*

Liza: *Please walk toward the back of the barn*

I am confused by her message. What could she possibly mean? I am hesitant, but make my way behind the barn. I slowly turn the corner and look around. I falter when I see it. I catch myself before I trip, falling to my knees at the sight of my old motorcycle. It looks practically brand new. I can tell it has been restored, and it looks phenomenal. The last time I checked, it was in the old barn under a tarp. My old Harley has a new paint job and wicked-looking tires. I rise to my feet and crank it up. I can hear that it has had a tune-up. I have a feeling I know who did the work. My heart is beating faster than it ever has. I worry it may burst from my chest, and then my cell phone dings again.

Liza: *Julia had been talking to Paul for weeks about restoring your motor-cycle. They formed a friendship while he was working on your bike. It was over the phone at the start.*

Liza: *She wanted to bring you back to life and to get you back on this bike. She wanted you to have your freedom again.*

Liza: *Paul and Julia hit it off through the restoration of your bike. They met at the bar to arrange for your bike to be delivered. Their love had been forming for weeks. Paul was going to bring the bike to you the next week, and Julia wanted him to meet you and the rest of your family.*

The last text did me in: I drop to my knees again. I am speech-less at the lengths my sister went to for me. The state of the bike shows how talented Paul was.

I drop my head as the emotions build. The love Julia put into this is overwhelming. I can almost hear her laughing because she knows I am admitting that she was right.

"I miss you like crazy and wish I could have you on the back of my bike, Sis. I promise I will cherish this gesture. I love you, Julia." I speak like she is right beside me.

My phone is still in my hand, and I say a silent prayer that Liza will respond if I text her.

Jackson: *Can I see you?*

Liza: *Why now?*

Jackson: *I miss you and need you!*

Liza: *I'm not available right now.*

I screwed up. I stand and walk to my bike, then finally sit on it. My nerves are raw, and I feel alive by being on this bike again. I wish Liza was here to share this moment with me. How did she make it all happen? I guess she got in contact with Will Greenfield from *Berkeley Bike and Restoration*. I need to drive to Berkeley Springs and pay Will a visit and thank him in person. I will plan a road trip soon.

I'm not sure how long I was sitting there on my bike before I heard the barn door open. I figure it is Dad or Mom coming to see how I am doing.

"Did you guys have a hand in helping Liza with this surprise?" I ask without looking up.

"They waited while Will unloaded the bike, but I handled all the rest."

I am caught off guard because it is Liza's voice I hear. The sound of her voice is pure heaven to me. I watch with anticipation as she walks to my side of the barn. She turns the corner and slowly strolls toward me. Time stops.

Liza is a vision to behold, with her long hair and lush lips. Her lips are glossy and seductive, and she is wearing a pair of dark jeans and her signature black boots. She has a dark green top and the silver necklace and earrings I liked from before. I've been in love with her all this time, and it hits me hard at this moment. I missed her so damn much.

She approaches and stands next to my bike.

"How are you?" she asks, and I can hear the nervousness in her voice.

"I can breathe now. I thought you were gone," I reply.

"My stuff is packed. This is my last stop before hitting the road." She smiles, nervously twisting her necklace. I don't let her stand there long. I reach out and pull her onto my lap. I catch her off guard, but she doesn't fight me. Holding her in my arms, I look directly into her eyes.

"What on earth are you doing?" she asks while holding my gaze. She probably thinks I have lost my mind, but I see the fire in her eyes.

CHAPTER

twenty-three

LIZA

I HADN'T DARED TO DREAM I would end up in Jackson's arms again.

"I was battling with my grief and had no idea you had been dealing with your dad's death. Can you please forgive me?" he asks as he holds me close. Reaching up, he gently pulls my mouth toward his.

He is breaking down my defenses, and I am okay with it. I have missed him.

Our hearts are pounding, and I feel like they are beating in rhythm. He whispers against my ear.

"Liza, I want you to be my forever. I love you with everything in me, but please tell me what you need and want." His breathing sounds shallow now in anticipation of my answer.

He holds me tight and keeps his face near mine. I didn't make him wait long.

"I want you as my forever, too. I love you with all my heart." I turn and put my lips on his. We lay against each other, his arms wrapped around me. Then my lips part, allowing his tongue to dip into my waiting mouth. He tastes better than I remember, and suddenly he lifts me on top of him. I wrap my legs around him as we sit on his bike.

"Are we safe both sitting on this bike?"

"I have us, and I promise not to let anything happen to you," he replies with a low, sexy, confident tone.

We sit on his bike and explore each other. Jackson cradles my face and continues to ravage my mouth. The electric current is firing strong right now. There is such a draw between us, and it is more than the lust it was in the beginning.

I feel safe being in his arms, and now I feel safe letting him be in my heart. I know we both have been broken and need to repair many pieces, but I think we can help each other do it. We have enough love together to help each other heal. This man sets me on fire, and I have to admit that being on this motorcycle is hotter than hell. I'm usually a total romantic, but now I'm feeling more lust-driven.

I shift and feel how hard he is, so I rub up and down on him for a little tease. He moans and takes my bottom lip between his teeth and holds it there for a few seconds. I love the sensation. He puts his lips fully back on mine.

"You have too many clothes on," he says with a laugh while still kissing me.

I ease off him and his motorcycle. Jackson doesn't take his eyes off me as I unzip my boots, and then slowly pull them off. He still watches as I unbutton my jeans and slide them down my legs. His eyes grow wide as he sees all I have on is a black thong.

"You better get that gorgeous backside up here," he growls and grabs my hips. I giggle and hop back on him and the bike. I was so busy doing my striptease that I missed him unzipping his jeans. I watch as he pulls himself free from his boxers. My man has magic hands.

He was rock hard and more than ready for me to climb on. I rise, and keep his mouth on mine, then lower my wet center down on his hard length. We move together, building a feverish pace on the seat of his Harley.

"I missed you so much," I whisper. He growls low and sexy in agreement. He brings his lips back onto mine, and kisses me like he is searching for lost treasure. He grinds his hips into my core and my climax builds. Grabbing my ass with both hands, he guides me up and down, sending shock waves through me. I lose myself to the moment and start to scream his name. He quickly kisses me and smothers the scream, but I feel every bit of the entire climax. It leaves me quivering.

"Liza, I am right with you, baby." Jackson's hands feel incredible on me. He moves me closer and puts his length deeper inside of my center. Jackson gives me a few more thrusts, and then I feel him shudder. He says my name, then wraps some of my hair around his hand, tugging as he gives one final thrust inside of me. We sit there for a minute and enjoy being in each other's arms. I want to stay right there forever.

"Please tell me what you are thinking about, beautiful," he says as he brushes the hair away from my face.

I hold his forearm, nervous about asking him the stories behind his tattoos, but I figure now is my chance.

"How long ago did you get all your tattoos? Do they hold any special meaning?" I run my hand down the tattoo sleeve and look up at him. Jackson hugs me tight.

"I didn't get my first tattoo until the day I enlisted in the Marines. The rest of my tattoos are stories related to people and places, or references to songs. They all hold a special meaning to me or represent a memory."

"It's amazing that you have these intricate life stories woven on this forever storyboard. I feel honored you would share them with me." I kiss him. "I also want to share another feeling with you; the feeling that your sister had her hand in us finding our way to each other." I stroke his arm along his tattoos.

He laughs. "I have to agree with you. I never would believe people can guide you on a journey, but I can't deny that Julia is involved in this one," Jackson replies. "I want you to know I was intrigued from the moment I found your beautiful face in the church."

"You could see me in the back?"

He nods. "I did, and I was drawn to you. My heart was broken, and I didn't want to sit through the service, but something made me look up, and there you were," he explains.

How crazy that we locked in on each other that day.

He smiles. "We need to get dressed before we're caught." He winks. I agree and move to get off of him and the bike.

As I am dressing, the old lonely feeling I used to feel is fading fast. I owe it all to a wild farm girl who I met in a bar one night. Julia helped me on a path of finding love and letting people love me. I know I deserve happiness, and I plan on making sure her legacy lives on.

EPILOGUE

SIX MONTHS LATER
JULIA'S SPOT. COSTELLO FARM. 3:00 P.M.

I T WAS JULIA'S FAVORITE PLACE, and I feel lucky that it's a place where we can keep a connection forever. Her parents placed a hand-carved bench made of barn wood on the same spot where we spread her ashes. It took her family six months to handle this emotional task, and the bench is situated on the overlook perfectly. You can see across the lake and the whole farm. I like to come here and enjoy the peace during sunrise each morning, but it also gives me the opportunity to talk with Julia.

I keep her updated on my life here on the farm and with her brother. We've recently moved in together. I love his house and its proximity to this bench. I am keeping my promise to carry on her legacy. The Costello's created a scholarship at Julia's high school in her name, and I get to be part of the committee to find other kids out there with the same passion for life as she had.

My photography business changed after the ribbon ceremony. Several local businesses loved the pictures I had on display and have commissioned me. I've been selling photos in the storefront, and the sales have been increasing each day. My focus has been on local photography. I keep weekends busy with requests for weddings, engagement photos, and birth announcements. I've got to admit, my favorite is the birth announcements.

Frankie keeps asking when Jackson and I will have our own engagement announcement. I love him deeply, but just moving into his house was a huge step. I talk with Julia often about her grandmother and the constant nudging toward marriage and babies. The equine therapy program is going great for Jackson. He is getting ready to advertise for a program assistant. He has a waiting list now, making it hard to manage all the students on his own.

We have been out for some long rides on his motorcycle. I never thought I would enjoy being on the back of it, but I love sitting behind Jackson and holding on to him. It gives you a feeling of freedom, exactly the way he described it to me. We made a trip to the bike shop where Paul worked and met the owner. Will mentioned that Gideon, Paul's brother, was coming back to town. Jackson told Will he would like to meet up with him to learn more about Paul, I guess in the same way I needed to know more about Julia.

Will shared with us that Paul's brother Gideon is the total opposite of him. He served in the military like Jackson, but we're not sure which branch or for how long. I sense there is a story surrounding Gideon, and my hope is that he will be willing to talk about his childhood and life with Paul. Jackson needs that final closure for sure.

I love living here in York. I never imagined I could be part of a real family. The night Julia walked into Dixon's bar was the best and worst night. I gained and lost my best friend in the same evening.

I want to do for others what Julia did for me. Maybe one day I can be like her and reach out to help someone who is lost and lonely in this world.

Julia, you will forever be missed, but your light will always shine.

THE END

AUTHOR'S
note

I WAS IN A BAR ONE night and met a complete stranger. She walked in and immediately I noticed this girl was wild and a free spirit. I spent the next few hours dancing and having fun with her. She recently moved to the area and hoping for a fresh start. She explained that she was on a blind date and had ridden to the bar on the back of his motorcycle.

Her story gave me the idea for *Bar Girl*. I often wonder if she is still with her blind date or has moved on to bigger and better things.

I hope you have a best girlfriend and if not, I wish you good luck in finding your Liza or Julia.

ACKNOWLEDGMENTS

Bar Girl was my first book. So many people helped keep me on course to make this book a reality. The first thank you has to go to my mom. She gave me my thirst for reading that still has not been quenched to this day. She unfortunately passed away before I finished this book. Thank you for always loving me!

To my family for supporting my childhood dream: my sister Sarah, thank you for being my first beta reader and giving me the toughest feedback. You made me a stronger writer and I love you even more for that. My boys, Lukas and Jakob, you inspire me every day to be a better mother and person. It always made my day when you asked me about my book. You both are rock stars! My nephew Grayson, you are the person I want to be when I grow up. I love you and feel blessed to be part of your life. Keep dreaming and asking questions about everything!

To my kick-ass beta readers: Charlie, Chelsea, Jeannie, Jodi, Kristy, Mac, Sam, Savannah, and Tina, thank you for giving me your honest feedback when I sent you a rough version of my story and was learning the process right along with you.

Chell and Tamara, thanks for holding my hand through the

editing process, and having patience during all my edits as a first time author.

To my amazing friends from *The Author Transformation Alliance:* You gave me the support and encouragement to write this book. When I attended my first writing retreat and sat among all these inspirational people, I thought I was out of my league. They never once made me feel that way. The best advice they gave me that weekend, "Just write. Put your words down on paper and worry about the editing process later." That saved me. It got me out of my head and into my story. Thank you!

My weekly pep-squad: Nydia and Lynne, you ladies are amazing! Thanks for listening each week during our author calls and showing such unwavering support. I had many low times this past year and without you two, I'm not sure I would have made it to the finish line.

To my mentor and friend, Audrey, there are not enough pages to tell you how much your support and encouragement has meant to me. You dreamed right along with me and gave me many virtual hugs during my writing process. I will forever be grateful that you pushed me along my journey when I was scared, sad, and broken. I never thought this would have been possible but you have a magic about you and I am so grateful you decided to spread a little my way. I love you and wish you all the happiness in the world.

Lastly, thanks to everyone who supported my dream and gave me encouragement.

Your words fueled my soul. I love you from the bottom of my heart.

ABOUT THE *author*

R.K. started sneaking peeks at her mom's romance novels before she hit middle school. She has always had her own stories in her head but never the courage to write them down. After one life changing writer's retreat, she began her journey. When she is not writing you can find her exploring with her camera or discovering new music. R.K. lives in Virginia with her two fantastic boys Lukas and Jakob.

f facebook.com/AuthorR.K.Fultz

⊙ instagram.com/r_k_fultz

www.ingramcontent.com/pod-product-compliance
Lightning Source LLC
Chambersburg PA
CBHW020309150626
46552CB00022B/2230